"I wanted to make sure you were feeling all right. Any fever?" Thorne asked.

"I don't think so. See for yourself," Charity said.

Thorne hesitated, then, looking into her eyes, he laid his hand on her forehead. "I think you're cool enough."

Charity blushed. She had never felt like this before. Was this what love felt like? Could she have been wrong to plan to lead a solitary life after she was widowed? Such a decision had seemed perfectly sensible at the time. Only now was it coming into question.

Her eyes searched the depths of Thorne's dark gaze. Was she imagining it, or was there truly a new tenderness in the way he looked at her?

Afraid he would deny such emotions, she simply smiled at him and said, "Thank you for looking after me."

Books by Valerie Hansen

Love Inspired Historical

Frontier Courtship
Wilderness Courtship

Love Inspired Suspense

*Her Brother's Keeper
The Danger Within
*Out of the Depths
Deadly Payoff
Shadow of Turning

*Serenity, Arkansas

Love Inspired

*The Wedding Arbor
*The Troublesome Angel
*The Perfect Couple
*Second Chances
*Love One Another
*Blessings of the Heart
*Samantha's Gift
*Everlasting Love
The Hamilton Heir
A Treasure of the Heart

VALERIE HANSEN

was thirty years old when she awoke to the presence of the Lord in her life and turned to Jesus. In the years that followed she worked with young children, both in church and secular environments. She also raised a family of her own and played foster mother to a wide assortment of furred and feathered critters.

Married to her high school sweetheart since age seventeen, she now lives in an old farm house she and her husband renovated with their own hands. She loves to hike the wooded hills behind the house and reflect on the marvelous turn her life has taken. Not only is she privileged to reside among the loving, accepting folks in the breathtakingly beautiful Ozark mountains of Arkansas, she also gets to share her personal faith by telling the stories of her heart for Steeple Hill's Love Inspired lines.

Life doesn't get much better than that!

VALERIE HANSEN
Wilderness Courtship

Steeple Hill®

Published by Steeple Hill Books™

STEEPLE HILL BOOKS

Steeple
Hill®

ISBN-13: 978-0-373-82793-0
ISBN-10:   0-373-82793-8

WILDERNESS COURTSHIP

Copyright © 2008 by Valerie Whisenand

www.SteepleHill.com

Printed in U.S.A.

"Assuredly, I say to you, inasmuch
as you did it to one of the least of these
my brethren, you did it to me."
—*Matthew* 25:40

To all the parents who continue struggling
to do the best they can and to those extraordinary
individuals who take in other people's children
and make them their own. It is truly a gift.

Prologue

New York, 1853

The wooden deck of the three-masted freighter *Gray Feather* rose and fell, rocked by the building swells. Thorne Blackwell knew a storm was imminent, he could smell its approach in the salty air, hear the anxiety in the calls of the soaring gulls and feel the changing weather in his bones. Pacing nervously, he awaited the arrival of his half brother, Aaron, and Aaron's family. Once they were safely aboard he'd relax. At least he hoped he would.

It had been over two years since Thorne had heard from Aaron, or any of the other Ashtons for that matter, and he wasn't quite sure what to expect. Would Aaron have contacted him if he hadn't been desperate? It was doubtful. Then again, Aaron had good reason for whatever misgivings he still harbored.

Thorne braced his feet apart on the pitching deck, pushed his hat down more tightly over his shoulder-length dark hair and drew up the collar of his woolen frock coat against the impending gale. Of all the nights for anyone to decide he needed immediate passage to San Francisco, this had to be the worst. Then again, Aaron's note had contained such evident panic, perhaps the risk was warranted. Thorne hoped so, since Naomi and the child would also be boarding.

Lying at anchor in the crowded New York harbor, the *Gray Feather* was fully loaded and awaiting final orders to embark on her third voyage around the horn. They'd hoist sail at dawn and be on their way, providing the storm didn't thwart their plans. Thorne had fought nature before. But for the grace of a benevolent God, he would have been a resident of Davy Jones's locker instead of the owner of the finest full-modeled vessel ever built in Eastport.

Why God had chosen to spare him from drowning at sea when so many of his comrades had lost their lives he didn't know. The only thing of which he was certain was his current role as his only sibling's protector.

Peering into the fog he spied a bobbing lantern in the prow of a small boat off the starboard. Shouting orders, he assembled members of the crew and affected a safe, though treacherous, boarding.

Aaron handed the sleepy two-year-old he was carrying to his wife, then shook Thorne's hand with vigor and obvious relief. "Thank you. I was afraid you might not want to help us. Not after the way we last parted."

Touched, Thorne hid his emotion behind a brusque facade. "Nonsense. Let's get you all inside before the rain begins in earnest. Then you can tell me everything."

He winced as his brother placed a protective arm around Naomi's shoulders. Her head was bowed over the blanket-wrapped child in her arms, her face hidden by the brim of her burgundy velvet bonnet, yet Thorne could see her golden hair as clearly as if they were once again walking hand in hand through a meadow and dreaming of an idyllic life together.

He set his jaw. Whatever else happened on this voyage, he was not going to resurrect a love better left dead. He and Naomi had had their chance at happiness, or so Thorne had thought, and she had chosen to wed Aaron, instead. That was all there was to it and all there ever would be. He had long ago concluded that romantic love was highly overrated and nothing had happened since to change his mind.

Guiding his guests into the captain's cabin he explained, "I've arranged for you to occupy these quarters until we can prepare a suitable suite elsewhere. It's not the quality you're used to, of course, but it's the best I could do on such short notice."

"It's fine," Aaron was quick to say as he ducked to guide his wife to a chair beneath a swaying lantern suspended from a beam. "I don't know how to thank you."

"All I ask is an explanation," Thorne replied. He leaned against the inside of the cabin's narrow door and crossed his arms. "What has happened to make you so insistent on leaving New York?"

Aaron's gaze darted to his wife, then rested lovingly on the small boy asleep in her lap. "It's mostly because of Jacob," he said sadly. "Father has grown more and more irrational as the years have passed. We think he may be going insane, although no doctors will agree to it and chance losing the exorbitant retainers he pays them. He's turned against us just the way he turned against you."

Thorne gave a deep-throated laugh. "I doubt that very much. At least he doesn't keep reminding you you're not really his son—or refuse to allow you to call yourself an Ashton."

"He may as well do so," his brother said. "He's made up his mind that my family is evil and has ordered me to divorce my wife and abandon my child."

"What?" Thorne's dark eyes narrowed. Unfolding his crossed arms, he removed his hat and raked his fingers through his thick, almost-black hair. "Why would he do that?"

"It's evident that his mind is unhinged. Some of the threats he's made lately are dire, indeed. There is no way I would consent to remain under his roof one more day, let alone subject my family to his lunatic ravings."

"I can understand that," Thorne said. "But why leave the city?"

"Because," Aaron said with a shaky voice, "if I won't agree to a divorce he has threatened to free me by having Naomi and my son killed."

Chapter One

San Francisco, 1854

Charity Beal stood on the board walkway outside the hotel, pulled a paisley shawl around her shoulders and raised her face to bask in the sun's warming rays. A mild breeze off the ocean ruffled wisps of pale blond curls that had escaped her neatly upswept hair and her blue eyes sparkled in the brightness of the day.

Smiling, she did her best to ignore the noise of the passing horses and wagons as she sighed and breathed deeply, enjoying the sweet, salt air. Thankfully, a recent shower had washed away most of the dust and dirt, yet hadn't left the streets too muddy for normal travel.

Spring days in the city by the bay were more often foggy than clear and Charity was loath to retreat back inside even though it was now her duty to assist Mrs.

Montgomery in the kitchen. Perhaps stealing a few more precious moments of sunshine would be all right, she told herself, appreciating the balmy weather yet cognizant of her place as part of the hotel staff.

The Montgomery House Hotel had been rebuilt of brick after its damage in the earthquakes and fires of 1850 and 1851, as had many of the other commercial buildings, including the Jenny Lind Theater. Few of the thousands of immigrants who crowded the city could afford to board at Montgomery House but those folks who did were usually well satisfied, especially since the rooms now contained real beds with feather ticking instead of the narrow, hanging cots of the previous structure.

Charity and her father, Emory Beal, had begun as tenants and had quickly decided to stay on. At least Emory had. As far as Charity was concerned she knew she could be happy anywhere as long as she remained a widow.

Remembrances of her cruel husband made her shiver in spite of the warmth of the day, and she drew her shawl more tightly against the inner chill. She knew it must be a terrible sin to celebrate anyone's death but she couldn't help being grateful that the Lord had seen fit to liberate her from her degrading marriage to Ramsey Tucker. Just the thought of that vile man touching her again made gall rise in her throat.

Shaking off the unpleasant memories and turning to reenter the hotel, Charity noticed a small group of people trudging up the hill from the direction of the wharf. Travelers of that class weren't often seen, yet it was the imposing gentleman in the lead who immediately caught and held her attention.

He reminded her of someone going to the gallows—or perhaps the hangman, himself—such was his aura. A short, black cape furled from the shoulders of his coat as he walked and he carried a silver-tipped cane. His Eastern-style felt hat had a narrow enough brim that she could easily discern his scowl and square jaw.

Trailing him were a man and woman holding the hands of a small child who struggled to keep up while walking between them. Their clothing was elegant and obviously expensively tailored but their countenance was as downtrodden as that of the poorest immigrant.

Charity hurriedly ducked through the doorway and had almost reached the visiting parlor when a deep, male voice behind her commanded, "Wait."

She whirled to face the dark-haired traveler she'd been surreptitiously studying. "Yes?"

Instead of approaching the desk where a young clerk awaited, the stranger removed his hat, bowed slightly and addressed her. "We require rooms. Can you vouch for the character of this establishment?"

She nodded. "Yes, sir. I certainly can."

"Have you stayed here often?"

"My father and I live here," she said. "If you choose to join us in the dining room for supper, you'll meet him. The evening meal is served at seven. Dinner is at one but as you can see—" she gestured toward the grandfather clock at the far end of the room "—you've missed it." She peered past him to smile at the weary child. "I can probably find a few cookies and a glass of cold milk if the little one is hungry."

"Jacob always enjoys a cookie," the pale, light-haired woman replied. "We would be obliged." She bent down to the boy's level and added, "Wouldn't we, son?"

He merely nodded, his eyes as wide and expressive as a frightened doe's.

Charity approached and offered the woman her hand. "I'm Miss Beal, please call me Charity. And you are…?"

"Naomi. This is my husband, Mr. Ashton." She shyly glanced toward the taller man who had proceeded to the clerk's station and was signing the register. "And that gentleman is his half brother, Mr. Thorne Blackwell."

Charity lowered her voice to ask, "Does he always order strangers around?"

Naomi's cheeks reddened. "A bit, I'm afraid. But his heart is in the right place. We've just come from a long sea voyage around the horn and we desperately need our rest."

"Then don't let me keep you," Charity said. "As soon as you're settled in your rooms, I'll bring young Master Jacob his cookies and milk."

She was taken aback when Naomi's husband clamped a hand on his wife's shoulder, shook his head and gave her a wordless look of warning.

Startled, Naomi immediately took Charity's hand and held it as if clasping a lifeline. "I spoke foolishly just now. Please, if anyone asks, you must swear you've not seen us. Promise me?"

"Of course, but…"

"I'll explain later."

"All right. I won't breathe a word."

The men hoisted their belongings and started up the stairs while Naomi balanced the child on her hip. Waiting until they were out of sight, Charity crossed to the desk clerk. "What names did that gentleman sign?"

The young man smirked as he spun the register book for her perusal. "Mr. Smith and Mr. Jones and family, if you choose to believe such tales."

"I see."

She checked their respective room numbers, then headed for the kitchen. So what if their new boarders were traveling incognito? That was often the case west of the Rockies. Here, a person could begin again without having to explain past sins. She should know. That was exactly what she'd been doing ever since her fateful journey from Ohio by wagon train with her sister, Faith.

Those had been the worst months of Charity's life, and although her loved ones had survived the ordeal, they all bore scars of some sort. Connell McClain, Faith's new husband, was scarred from encounters with the Cheyenne, and poor Faith had nursed broken ribs during the latter part of the arduous trek.

Charity's scars didn't manifest themselves physically. They were deeper, in her heart and soul, and the ache of her personal tribulation and loss remained so vivid the remembrances still gave her nightmares.

Nevertheless, she didn't want those memories to fade. She wanted to remember precisely how foolish she'd once been so that she would never, ever, be tempted to make the same mistakes again.

Thorne closed the door to his brother's room and stood with his back to it as he faced Naomi. "What did you say to that woman downstairs?" he demanded.

Tears softened her already pale blue eyes. "I'm so sorry. I know you cautioned us to use fictitious names but I haven't spoken to another lady in months and the truth just slipped out. Charity won't betray us. She promised she wouldn't."

He muttered under his breath. "What good is all the trouble we've gone to if you don't remember to hide your real identities?"

Placing a sheltering arm around his wife's slim shoulders Aaron stood firm. "She said she was sorry, Thorne. What's done is done. I'm sure a simple hotel maid isn't smart enough to engage in subterfuge."

"Hah! Any fool could see that that woman is no simpleton. Nor is she a maid. She said she and her father are hotel guests, not staff, so don't discount her capabilities or count on her loyalty."

Weeping, Naomi knelt to draw the boy into her

embrace while Aaron began to pace the floor of the small, sparsely furnished bedroom.

"Don't worry," Thorne said firmly. "I'll take care of it. If the woman can't be reasoned with, she can probably be bribed or threatened."

"You sound just like Father!" Aaron blurted.

Thorne's eyes narrowed and his countenance darkened with barely repressed anger. "Never say that again, do you hear? I won't be compared with that man. He's *your* father, not mine."

"But you've obviously learned from him," the younger man countered.

"No. I've learned from years on my own and from the writings of my *real* father." Noting the shock on Aaron's face, he went on. "Are you surprised? I was. Shortly before I left home, Mother told me all about her brief marriage to my late father and where I might locate the rest of the Blackwell family."

"Did you?"

"Yes, eventually. I didn't seek out my grandfather until I'd spent a few years at sea and felt I'd proved myself." *And had faced death more than once.* "Grandfather and I didn't have much time together before he died but we got along very well. He gave me my father's journal, as well as willing me enough money to buy into a partnership on my first freighter."

"So that's how you became successful."

"No," Thorne countered, "I could have squandered my inheritance in any number of ways. The investments I made, instead, were based on my experience at sea, not on mere wishful thinking. I knew exactly what I was doing and lived frugally. That's what I was trying to explain when I returned to New York three years ago. But no one would listen to me, not even you."

Thorne noted Aaron's pained expression. It was during that short visit that Thorne had met and fallen in love with Naomi but she had chosen to wed the younger brother, presumably because Aaron was in line to inherit the Ashton fortune.

Squaring his shoulders, Thorne faced him. "Forget the past. It's your future that counts. Leave the details to me. We've come this far together and I'll see to it that your foolish mistakes don't sink our ship, so to speak."

Naomi raised her reddened face to him, tears glistening on her cheeks, and whispered, "Thank you."

It was all Thorne could do to keep from tempering his harsh expression as he gazed at her. She was suffering for her poor choices and for that he was sorry, but, as he had finally realized when he'd encountered her again, any tender feelings he had once harbored were long gone and he was therefore loath to display any tenderness that might mislead her.

If anything good came out of this fiasco, perhaps it was that it had finally freed his heart from the fetters of unrequited love and had given him a chance to make amends with his brother over almost stealing his betrothed.

* * *

Charity was climbing the stairs, one hand raising the hem of her calico frock and apron as she stepped, the other balancing a glass of milk on a plate with two freshly baked cookies. As she neared the landing, a shadow fell over her.

Her head snapped up. The mysteriously intriguing stranger blocked her path. "Oh! You startled me."

Thorne didn't give way.

"Excuse me, please," Charity said politely. "I have some treats to deliver."

"I'll take that for you."

As he reached for the small plate she held it away. "No need. I can manage nicely."

"But you're a guest here. You shouldn't be doing chores."

That brought a smile. "Actually, I started out as a guest about a year ago when my father decided to move to San Francisco. Since then, I've taken a part-time position helping the proprietress, Mrs. Montgomery, to pay for Papa's and my room and board."

One dark eyebrow arched as he said, "Really? I would have thought, considering the dearth of eligible women in these parts, you'd have found yourself a suitably rich husband by now."

She could feel the warmth rising to redden her cheeks. "You assume a lot, sir."

"My apologies if I've offended you," Thorne said as he stepped aside and gestured. "After you."

Spine stiff, steps measured, Charity led the way to

the room the family occupied. Behind her she could sense the imposing presence of the man Naomi had called Thorne. He was well named, Charity decided, since he was definitely a thorn in her side—probably to everyone he met. Clearly he was used to getting his own way. Equally as clearly, he was not used to being challenged by anyone, let alone a woman.

He placed his hand on the knob of the door she sought and stood very still.

"May I?" she asked boldly.

"In a moment. First, I must ask for your discretion, particularly regarding my brother's family. We're traveling in secret and must therefore guard our true identities judiciously."

Charity's chin jutted out, her head held high. "And your point is?"

"Simply that we require your silence. Since you're a working woman, perhaps a generous gift would help you forget you ever saw us."

She drew herself up to her full height of five and a half feet, noting that the top of her head, even piled high with her blond curls, barely came to the man's shoulder. Nevertheless, she was determined to give him a piece of her mind. How *dare* he try to bribe her!

"Sir," she said fervently, "I have promised Naomi that I would keep her secret and so I will, but it is because *she* asked me for my silence, not because your money interests me in the slightest. Is that clear?"

Thorne bowed from the waist as he said, "Perfectly."

"Good. Because there is a hungry, tired little boy

waiting for this food and no bully in a fancy brocade vest is going to stop me from delivering it to him. Am I making myself understood?"

A slight smile started to twitch at the corners of his mouth and Charity couldn't decide whether or not he was about to laugh at her. Since she didn't want to spill the milk, she sincerely hoped she was not going to have to balance it and slap his face at the same time for unseemly behavior.

His dark eyes glistened as the smile developed. To Charity's dismay she found him quite handsome when he wasn't frowning or trying to appear so menacing.

Averting her gaze she nodded toward the closed door. "May I go in?"

"Of course." He rapped twice, then paused a moment before opening the door for her and standing back to let her pass.

The child had already fallen asleep on the bed. Aaron stood facing the only window, staring into the street below. Naomi was the only one who looked happy to see Charity. She smiled. "Oh, thank you!"

"It's my pleasure. I'll leave this plate on the dresser for your son when he wakes," Charity said, speaking quietly. "There's fresh water in the ewer on the washstand. Is there anything else I can do for you?"

She noted Naomi's nervous glance toward Thorne and sought to ease her fears. "The gentleman and I have come to an understanding, so there's nothing to fret about."

Naomi looked as if she were about to weep with relief.

"Rest well," Charity continued. "I see the men have pocket watches but we also ring a gong for supper so you'll know when to join us, regardless. Please do." She eyed the woman's tailored traveling outfit. "And there's no need to dress. What you're wearing is most appropriate."

"Thank you." Naomi sniffled. "For everything."

"It was my pleasure to be able to assist you," Charity said formally. Stepping closer so she could speak without being easily overheard, she added, "And don't give that thorny brother-in-law of yours another thought. He doesn't scare me one bit."

From behind her a deep voice said, "I heard that."

Charity whirled and found him grinning at her. "Good," she said, hands fisted on her hips. "Because the sooner you and I understand each other, the better I'll like it."

"I wasn't trying to intimidate or insult you, madam. I guess I'm too used to dealing with rough seamen."

"Apparently." Charity boldly stood her ground. "Listen, Mr. whatever-your-name-is-today, you may be used to having your own way but you can't hold a candle to some of the folks I've dealt with since leaving Ohio."

Like my late husband, she added to herself. After living through that dreadful marriage and the abuses she had suffered during the journey to California, there wasn't much that frightened her. Not anymore.

She started past Thorne toward the open door, then paused to add, "You may be a tad overbearing but I can tell you're not evil. Believe me, I know *exactly* what that kind of man looks like."

The flabbergasted expression on Thorne's face was fleeting and he quickly regained his usual staid composure as she swept past and left the room.

Although Charity couldn't begin to guess the plight of the little family, she vowed to add them to her daily prayers. Clearly, they were embroiled in some kind of trouble, perhaps dire, and her kind heart insisted she help in some way. If they wouldn't allow her to render physical assistance she'd simply bring them before her Heavenly Father and let Him do what He would.

A benevolent God had carried her and her sister through many terrible trials and she knew He wouldn't abandon an innocent little boy and his sweet mother.

The stranger stood outside on the walkway and lit up a cigar. Now that he'd spotted his quarry and knew where they were staying, there was no rush. On the contrary. Given the pleasures of San Francisco's wilder side he was going to enjoy this part of his assignment. He'd simply post a guard to make sure the Ashtons didn't leave without his knowledge and stop by to check on their status from time to time. Then, if it looked as if they were going to travel on, he'd be able to follow without being recognized. If not, there would be plenty of opportunity to rent a room at the Montgomery House and take care of business from the inside.

Either way, he and his cohorts couldn't fail.

Chapter Two

Fashions of the time dictated that both boys and girls wore dresses until the former reached the age of about six. Since Naomi had also chosen to keep her son's curly dark hair long, it occurred to Thorne that it might be safer to try to pass him off as a girl. Aaron would probably object, of course, but the more Thorne considered the idea, the more it appealed.

He broached the subject as he joined Aaron and the others to go downstairs to supper. "Jacob is awfully pretty for a boy," he said, smiling and patting the top of the child's head. "I think it would be safer if we called him Jane, for a while, don't you?"

As expected, his brother bristled with indignation. "I disagree completely. Think of how confusing that would be, especially for him. We can call him anything you want as long as he remains all boy."

Thorne shrugged. "Very well. Have it your way. I was just trying to protect you. Jacob is a common enough name so we may as well continue to use it."

"Don't worry. We'll be fine as soon as we reach Naomi's parents in Oregon Territory. They'll take care of him—and of us."

"Missionaries? How much protection can you expect from pacifists?"

"Just because Mr. and Mrs. White practice what they preach doesn't mean they'd allow any harm to come to us. Besides, they're well acquainted with the natives and settlers on both sides of the border. No strangers will be able to sneak up on their mission without arousing suspicion."

"I hope you're right," Thorne said soberly. "I heard there was an Indian uprising near there."

"I assume you're referring to the Whitman massacre?"

"Yes."

"That occurred seven or eight years ago. Things have settled down considerably since that unfortunate misunderstanding. You can't blame the Indians. They were fed erroneous information about Dr. Whitman and acted on it because they didn't understand how measles was spread. Besides, those were the Cayuse and Umatilla. The tribes Naomi's parents minister to are farther north, around Puget Sound. I understand they're quite accommodating."

Naomi chimed in. "That's right. The Nisqually and Puyallup leaders have actually helped my father in his dealings with less civilized tribes. Mama told us in her letters."

"If you say so." Thorne wasn't about to argue with her and give her more reason to worry. Whatever she and Aaron decided to do next was no concern of his. He'd gotten them safely as far as San Francisco and that was all they had asked of him. Still, he had grown attached to their winsome child during the long, tedious voyage and he could tell the boy liked him, too. It was Jacob's future that concerned him most.

He felt a tiny hand grasp one of his fingers as he started down the stairs. He smiled at the boy in response. Of all his relatives, Jacob was the one to whom he felt closest. Theirs was a strangely intuitive bond that had begun almost as soon as Aaron and Naomi had boarded the *Gray Feather* and had deepened as time had passed. Jacob had seemed unusually bright for a two-year-old, as well as curious almost to a fault and Thorne had taught him a lot about the workings of the ship during the long sea voyage. To his chagrin, he had to admit he was really going to miss the youngster when they parted.

Looking up, he noticed that their approach had drawn the attention of the young woman he had infuriated earlier. He greeted her politely as he and the boy reached the bottom of the stairs. "Good evening, ma'am."

"Good evening." She offered her right hand, then smiled and withdrew it when she noticed that his was being firmly controlled by his diminutive nephew. "Looks as if the nap helped."

"Resting has certainly improved *my* outlook," Thorne said. "Again, I must apologize for unintentionally offending you."

"No apology is necessary," Charity said. As the man and boy passed her, Jacob reached for her hand, grabbed her index finger tightly, and kept them together by tugging her along, too.

Charity laughed softly. "I see someone in your family likes me."

"Apparently. If you'll forgive my saying so, the boy has excellent taste. You look lovely this evening."

"Thank you, sir."

Noting the soft blush on her already rosy cheeks and the shy way she smiled, then averted her gaze, Thorne was confused. He had pictured this woman as a stiff, bossy matron, yet now she was acting more like an ingenue. Truth to tell, he didn't imagine she was more than nineteen or twenty years old. Still, by the time he was that age he had sailed around the horn more than once and had considered himself any man's equal.

Leading them to the table, Charity made brief introductions without citing all the travelers' names. "Those gentlemen over there are new guests, too," she said. "They're from Virginia and Pennsylvania, I believe. And this is my father, Emory Beal." She indicated a thin, gray-haired man at the far end of the rectangular dining table. "Next to him is Mrs. Montgomery. She owns this hotel and several other buildings along Montgomery Street."

The round-faced, portly woman grinned and patted her upswept, salt-and-pepper hair. "Land sakes, girl. You make me sound like a land baron. I'd of had more to brag on if the storm last November hadn't carried off sixty feet of the wharf at Clark's Point. That was pitiful."

"I'd heard about that damage," Thorne said. "I'm sorry the losses were yours."

"Well, these things happen," the proprietress said with a shrug. "Lately I've been concentrating on improvements to this here property. I reckon we'll have coal gas lamps to brag on soon, just like the Oriental Hotel and the Metropolitan Theater. Can't let the competition get ahead of me. No, sirree."

Thorne agreed. "Exactly the reason I've chosen the most modern sailing ships. We've already seen steam travel on a single vessel as far as the Isthmus of Panama. Someday I hope to be sending my own steamers all the way around the horn."

"My, my, you don't say."

"Yes, ma'am, I do."

Thorne stepped aside to shake hands with Emory while he waited for Aaron to seat his little family. That left Thorne with only one available chair, which happened to place him next to Jacob. Charity was already seated on the boy's left.

The other guests, all men, nodded brief greetings but were clearly more concerned with dishing up their share from the bowls and platters already on the table than they were with making polite conversation.

Thorne was about to reach for a nearby plate of sliced beef when he saw Charity clasp her hands, bow her head and apparently begin to pray. Since the hotel proprietress had not led any blessing on the food, he saw no reason to join in until he noticed that Jacob had folded his little hands in his lap and closed his eyes, too.

All right, Thorne decided. He was a big enough man to let a woman and child lead him, at least in this instance. Following suit he sat quietly and watched the young woman out of the corner of his eye until she stopped whispering and raised her head. He was about to reach over and tuck a napkin into Jacob's collar to serve as a bib when Charity did just that.

"I can manage him," Thorne said.

"It's no bother. He's a sweet child. So well mannered. He reminds me of my own nephew."

"You have family here?" Thorne asked as he plopped a dollop of mashed potatoes onto the boy's plate.

"My sister and her family live over near Sacramento City," she answered. "It was just chosen as the official state capitol to take the place of Benicia, you know." She looked to the child seated next to her. "Would you like some gravy?"

Thorne answered, "Yes, thanks."

That brought a demure laugh from Charity. "I was talking to my short friend here. I'll gladly ladle some over your potatoes, too, if you'd like."

"I think I can handle it myself," Thorne said with a lopsided grin. "But thank you for offering."

"You're quite welcome." She began to cut the slab of roast beef on her plate, then paused. "This piece is very tender. May I give him a little of it?"

"Of course. He doesn't like much, though. And cut it into very small bites."

"Believe it or not, I know how to feed a child."

"We should be doing that," Naomi said from across the table. "If you want to send him over, he can sit on my lap and eat from my plate."

Judging by the firm way the boy was grasping his fork and leaning his chin on the edge of the table, Thorne knew that Naomi's suggestion was not to his liking. "He's fine where he is. A little variety is good for him. And I promise we won't spoil him too badly."

"Speak for yourself, sir," Charity gibed. "I plan to enjoy my supper companion to the utmost."

When she smiled at the child, Thorne was astounded at how young and lovely she appeared. Her hair glistened like sunbeams on fine, golden silk and her eyes were as blue as a cloudless, equatorial, summer sky. It was as if the presence of the boy had lightened her usual burdens and given her a new lease on life. And Jacob had taken to her, as well, he noted. The two were acting as if they had always known each other.

Pensive, Thorne glanced at his brother and Naomi. Their countenance was anything but joyful by contrast. Aaron was eyeing the strangers at the table, looking ready to leap upon the first one who might pose a threat, while Naomi appeared near tears, as she had been during most of their sea journey. The one time Thorne had tried to discuss her concerns with her she had merely said that she feared for the lives of her dear ones.

He couldn't argue with that grim conclusion. Not if Aaron's words were to be believed. Louis Ashton had never been much of a father to either of them, nor had he been a kind, loving husband to the dear mother they shared. For that, alone, Thorne had grown to detest the man.

When Louis's last beating had raised welts on Thorne's sixteen-year-old shoulders, he had gone to his mother and begged her to leave the Ashton estate with him. Of course she had refused. But that was the night she had opened her heart and explained her painful past, including revealing her fears regarding the untimely demise of her first husband and her growing suspicion that Louis Ashton might have somehow been responsible.

Rather than be too specific, she had likened the tale to the biblical saga of King David and Bathsheba with Thorne's real father playing the part of the hapless Uriah. From there on, however, the basic facts of the story had diverged. Louis had rushed the new widow Blackwell into marriage and had gotten more than he'd bargained for a mere six months later. He'd gotten Thorne, another man's son, and he'd never forgiven the boy for being born.

At sixteen, Thorne had wanted to take Aaron with him and run away to sea but Mother had convinced him otherwise. Once he had entered that occupation and realized what a hard life he was facing as a young seaman, he was glad he had listened to her wisdom, at least in regard to his baby brother.

Yet look at him now, Thorne thought. Everything Aaron had hoped and planned for was ruined. He had no home, no source of income and no plans for the future other than to elude any assassins Louis might send in pursuit. It was a terrible, dangerous existence that faced the little family.

Thorne had known in his heart that he could not simply abandon Aaron in San Francisco and hope that he and his loved ones eventually managed to reach Naomi's parents in the Northern territories. Now that he thought about it in detail he knew what he had to do. Like it or not, he must accompany them. And in order to do that he had to transfer some of his business duties to underlings or risk financial disaster before he could return.

Having decided, he addressed his brother. "I know you're in a hurry to be on your way but I will need several more days to arrange my affairs before I can travel. The telegraph only connects to a few cities close by so I shall have to handle my business mostly with personal dispatches. Nevertheless, I think I can have everything settled by next Friday. How does that sound?"

Aaron's mouth gaped. "You're going with us?"

"Yes. If you have no objection."

"No, I…" He looked to his wife. "If it's all right with Naomi."

She merely nodded, her eyes misting.

"Good," Thorne said. "We'll need to keep our rooms a little longer than planned, Mrs. Montgomery. I trust that won't be a problem?"

"Not at all," the proprietress said cheerfully as she pushed back her chair and arose. "Save room for dessert. Our Charity baked two delicious apple pies this afternoon and I think they're almost cool enough to serve. I'll run and fetch 'em."

Watching the matron scurry away, Thorne wondered how such delicate hands as Charity Beal's could have spent much time in the kitchen, let alone have fashioned a pie worth eating. When he was served his portion and tasted it, however, he almost purred.

"Mmm, this is delicious. Are you sure Miss Beal really made it?"

The young woman bristled. "I beg your pardon? Are you insinuating that I would lie?"

Thorne couldn't help chuckling in response. "No, ma'am. I wouldn't dream of suggesting such a thing. I was just so impressed with your culinary prowess I was momentarily at a loss for words."

"Ha! That will be the day," she said. "It has been my experience that you have plenty of words for every occasion, sir, whether they are warranted or not."

Across the table, Emory Beal broke into cackles. "Atta girl, Charity. You tell him."

Thorne was laughing so heartily he covered his mouth with his napkin and nearly choked on his bite of pie.

When he glanced around at his fellow diners, however, he was struck by the taciturn expressions on some of the other guests' faces. It appeared that several of the younger men were particularly upset with him, perhaps because they had their sights set on wooing Charity Beal. Not that he blamed them. If he were seeking a wife, she would certainly be worth a second look.

Later, when Emory cornered him and thanked him privately for lifting the girl's spirits and helping to restore her gumption, he was so surprised he truly was at a loss for words. According to her father's insinuations, Charity had been through some unspeakable experiences which had caused her to become withdrawn and often to brood.

Thorne had no idea how his presence had elevated her mood but he was nevertheless glad to hear of the improvement. He liked her. And so did Jacob, which was even more important. The poor boy had been through plenty already and their arduous journey was far from over. A little sunshine in his short life was certainly welcome and the woman who had cheerfully provided it ranked high on Thorne's list of admirable people.

In the street outside the hotel, a small group of men had gathered to discuss the situation.

"They're leaving in a few more days," the tallest, youngest one said. "That means we have a little more time to plan."

There was a murmur of agreement before their portly, red-haired leader spoke. "We won't need much. We'll move tonight."

"What do you want me to do?"

"Slip this note under Ashton's door, then leave the rest to us." He handed a folded slip of paper to his wiry cohort and glanced at the other two burly men who were standing by waiting for their orders. "Just make sure you're not seen when you do it."

"I have the room just down the hall from them. Nobody will catch me. Is that all?"

"Yes." He started away. "And if you see any of us on the street afterward, you don't know us. Is that clear?"

"Perfectly."

"Good. Now go back inside and try to act natural. The hardest part will be over by morning."

Charity couldn't sleep. After tossing and turning for what seemed like hours, she arose, pulled on a lawn wrapper and tied the sash before she peeked out the door of her room to be sure no one else was up and about. The hallway was deserted.

She quickly lit a small oil lamp and tiptoed to the stairs, intending to help herself to one of the leftover cookies in the kitchen. She paused to listen intently. There were no sounds coming from any of the rooms except for Mrs. Montgomery's familiar, loud snoring at the far end of the hotel.

Proceeding, Charity was halfway down the staircase when she overheard muffled voices and stopped in her tracks. It sounded as if the parties involved were in the sitting room, which meant that her path to the kitchen was blocked unless she chose to dart around the newel post at the ground floor and hope her passage down the side hallway went unseen.

That idea didn't please her one iota. Dressed in a floor-length white wrapper and carrying a lit lamp, there was no way she wouldn't be noticed.

She was still standing there, trying to decide what to do, when one of the parties below raised his voice.

"I'm not going back with you," he said.

A response that sounded like a growl followed.

"No," the initial speaker replied. "It's not open to discussion. You won't harm me. You don't dare. Now get out of here."

This time, the growling voice was intelligible. "I have my orders and I aim to carry them out."

Charity wished she were back in her room, blissfully sleeping, but curiosity held her rooted to the spot. She did have the presence of mind to dim her lamp and cup her hand loosely around the glass chimney, however.

Soon there was the reverberation of a smack, followed by a heavy thud. Her heart began to hammer. It sounded as if someone—or something—had fallen.

Furniture scraped across the bare floors. Glass broke, or perhaps it was crockery, she couldn't tell which. There was more stomping and crashing around just before the rear door slammed.

Afraid to move, she waited and listened. All she could hear was the rapid pounding of her heart and the shallow rasping of her breath.

Above her, a second door opened and closed. Footfalls echoed hollowly on the wooden floor. She sensed another presence on the stairs.

Someone grabbed her arm before she could turn and look. She started to scream. A hand clamped over her mouth and a male voice, a familiar voice, ordered, "Hush."

Recognizing that it was Thorne, Charity nodded and he eased his hold. Instead of trying to explain what was going on she merely pointed in the direction of the parlor.

"Shush," Thorne hissed in her ear. "Stay here."

Grasping the banister she watched him descend as gracefully and quietly as a cat. He crouched, then whipped around the corner and disappeared.

In moments he returned. He had tucked the tails of his nightshirt into his trousers and was pulling his braces over his shoulders. "There's no one there now," he assured her. "I'm sorry if I frightened you. What's going on?"

"I don't know." She was trembling like a silly child, but couldn't seem to hold the lamp still even by using two hands. "I was hungry so I came down to get a cookie. The ground floor was dark. I heard voices. It sounded like an argument."

"*Men* arguing?" Thorne asked.

"Yes. Two of them, I think. There was something rather familiar about one and the other was almost too faint to hear. I thought he sounded very menacing, though. I suppose I was just nervous because I expected to be alone."

"What did they say?"

"Nothing much. One was talking about having a job to do and the other told him he wouldn't dare, or some such nonsense. They sounded like two school-yard bullies."

"Then what?"

She shrugged. "I don't know. I couldn't see a thing from up here on the stairway. I guess there was a fight but it was over so quickly I'm not certain. I did think I heard dishes breaking just before the door slammed."

"There is some damage in the kitchen but the place is deserted, now." His dark eyes suddenly widened and he dashed past her to continue climbing, taking the steps two at a time.

Charity followed him straight to his brother's room where he began to pound on the door.

"Aaron! Open up. Now."

"Hush. You'll wake every guest in the hotel," Charity warned.

Instead of heeding her admonition Thorne grabbed her lamp, then kicked the door and broke the lock away from the jamb. He held the light high, illuminating a circle that encompassed most of the small room.

In the center of the glow, Charity saw Naomi sitting in bed and clutching covers that were drawn up to her neck. Beside her, the exhausted toddler barely stirred in spite of the ruckus.

"Where's Aaron?" Thorne demanded.

"I don't know. Someone slipped a note under our door. Aaron read it and said he had to go out." Naomi began to sniffle. "I begged him to stay here with me but he insisted."

"What note. Where is it?"

"I—I think he put it in his coat pocket and took it with him. Why? What's happened?" Her breath caught. "Is, is he…"

"Dead?" Thorne muttered under his breath. "I doubt it. But I don't think he's in the hotel anymore, either. I strongly suspect he's been kidnapped."

Naomi gasped. "Are you sure?"

"Relatively. I explored the whole ground floor and he wasn't down there. Nobody was."

"I'll wake Papa and send him to fetch the sheriff," Charity said from the hallway. "We'll search everywhere. We'll find him."

In her heart of hearts she hoped and prayed she was right. If Aaron remained on land there was a fair chance they would be able to locate him, especially since San Francisco was rather isolated by the surrounding hills. If he had been taken aboard one of the many vessels coming and going by sea, however, he could already be out of their reach.

It was a frightening realization. It was also the most logical escape route for anyone wanting to effect a successful kidnapping!

Chapter Three

Thorne finished dressing, pulled on his coat and joined Emory Beal as he hurried from the hotel.

"I don't know where to start looking for the law, do you?" Thorne asked the older man.

"I've got a sneakin' suspicion where the sheriff'll be," Emory replied. "Follow me."

They made their way up Sacramento Street and located the lawman holding court with the mayor and half the city council in the What Cheer House saloon. A large crowd was toasting the previous day's groundbreaking ceremonies at Presidio Hill for the soon-to-be-built municipal water system and everyone seemed to be having a wonderful time drinking and eating the free food offered at the bar. A pall of smoke hung low in the stuffy room.

Thorne was glad that Emory was with him because the older man was well-known and was therefore able to readily convince the celebrants to form a vigilance committee and join in the search for Aaron.

Leaving the saloon in the company of dozens of inebriated, raucous men, Thorne jumped up on the edge of a watering trough and grabbed a porch support post for balance while he waved and shouted to command everyone's attention.

"There will be a large reward for my brother's return," he yelled, pleased to hear a responsive rumbling of excitement in the crowd. "He's a city fellow from New York so you should be able to pick him out from amongst the prospectors and immigrants. He was wearing a brown suit and vest. His hair is lighter than mine and he's a little shorter. He has no beard or mustache. If any of you spot him, I can be reached through the Montgomery House Hotel or the freighter *Gray Feather.* She's moored close to the main pier. Let's go, men. Time is of the essence."

Stepping down, he started off with the others. He would have preferred to head a sober search party but under the present circumstances he figured he was fortunate to have found a group of able-bodied men awake and willing to help at this time of night.

"It's all Chinese down that way," Emory told him, pointing. "Your brother'd stick out like a sore thumb in that neighborhood. The sheriff said he wants us to check the wharf while he and some of the others look in the gambling and fandango houses we still have. Come the first of April, bawdy houses'll be banned on Dupont, Jackson and Pacific. Don't know what this city's comin' to."

"All right," Thorne said. "I probably know the waterfront as well as most of the folks who live here."

"Been a sailor all your life?"

"In a matter of speaking." Thorne didn't think this was an appropriate time to mention that he had long since graduated from employee to employer. Nor was it a good idea to flaunt his wealth in a town with a reputation for lawlessness and greed, mainly thanks to the gold rush. San Francisco had come a long way from the canvas and board shacks he remembered from 1850 but it still hadn't managed to attain anything resembling the degree of civility Aaron and Naomi were used to back in New York.

Although Thorne's clothing bespoke a full purse, his actual worth far exceeded the external evidence. And that was the way he wanted it. He'd found out the hard way that if a man had money there was always someone eager and willing to separate him from it, one way or another. That much, he *had* learned from Louis Ashton.

The difference was what lay in a man's heart, not what lined his pockets, Thorne reminded himself. He would gladly pay whatever it took to get his brother back and not miss a penny of that money. Unfortunately, if Louis's hired thugs were responsible for the abduction, he feared that Aaron's freedom was not going to be for sale at any price.

* * *

Although Charity had wanted to join in the search, she knew better than to venture out onto the streets unescorted, especially after dark, so she had stayed behind to try to comfort Naomi.

By dawn the poor woman had sobbed herself into exhaustion and had finally fallen asleep. Although Charity was weary, too, she took pity on Jacob and kept him beside her while she did her morning chores and helped prepare breakfast for the remaining hotel guests.

Fortunately, the current Montgomery Hotel didn't house as many souls as it had before being rebuilt. Now that they were able to offer private rooms, the income from the establishment had improved while the workload had lessened. For that, Charity was doubly thankful. She didn't begrudge her father his ease but she sometimes did wish he'd contribute more to their daily necessities.

She shook off the negative feelings and reminded herself that she was blessed to have a roof over her head and to be in the company of a papa who loved and forgave her in spite of her folly as a younger woman. That she had survived at all was a wonderment. That she and Faith had both managed to locate their father and work together for the common good was almost miraculous, given the hardships and dangers they had faced.

Jacob had been gripping a handful of Charity's skirt ever since she had awakened and dressed him and she had allowed it because he seemed so determined, so needy. She felt him give her apron a light tug. Smiling, she looked down and asked, "Are you hungry, dear?"

The little boy nodded and her smile grew. What a darling. The depths of his chocolate-brown eyes sparkled and his thick, dark lashes would have been the envy of any girl.

Leading him to a table in the kitchen she lifted him onto a chair and said, "My, what a big boy you are. You sit here and I'll fetch your breakfast before we serve the others so you can eat first. Would you like that?"

Again he nodded and grinned, showing even, white teeth and dimples.

"You're spoiling that child," Annabelle Montgomery said as she kneaded dough on the opposite end of the table. "Not that I blame you. He's a cute one, all right. And such a little man. So brave, what with his…" She broke off and glanced at the ceiling.

"Yes, I know," Charity answered. "I've explained that his mama is ailing. Jacob is going to stay with me today so she can rest."

"Good idea. I don't suppose he'd like some flapjacks and homemade jam."

The little boy's head nodded so hard his dark curls bounced.

"My, my," the proprietress said, "looks like he just might. While this dough rises a bit I'll run out to the spring house and fetch some cool milk."

"I should do that for you," Charity said.

"Not this morning. You're needed here."

Annabelle's gentle gaze rested on the child and she shook her head slowly, sadly. "Perhaps we'll hear from our Emory soon and we can all relax. I've been prayin' hard ever since he left."

"So have I." Laying her hand atop the boy's head Charity stroked his silky hair. "I meant for Papa to find the sheriff and then come home but I should have known he'd want to stay and help in the search. I just worry about him, that's all."

"So do I," the portly proprietress said.

To Charity's amazement she thought she glimpsed moisture in Annabelle Montgomery's eyes as the other woman wheeled and left the room.

Thorne returned with Emory several hours later. Charity had set aside biscuits, as well as extra servings of ham and a bowl of red-eye gravy, assuming they'd be famished when they finally came home.

She was seated in a rocker in the hotel parlor, Jacob asleep in her arms, when the two men walked in.

Thorne approached her while Emory headed upstairs.

"Did you find your brother?" she asked.

"No. The sheriff is still keeping an eye open but there was no sign of him in any of the usual places."

"I'm so sorry."

"Yeah. Me, too."

"There are plates of food waiting for you and Papa in the warming oven over the stove," she said, continuing her slow, steady rocking. "I'd get up and serve you but as you can see, I'm otherwise occupied."

Thorne's overall expression was weary, yet a slight smile lifted the corners of his mouth. "Poor Jacob's probably as tired as the rest of us," he said, gazing fondly at the child. "I don't know what we're going to tell him about all this."

"I wouldn't say anything, for now," Charity suggested. "He's too young to understand the details and I don't see any reason to upset him needlessly."

"How's Naomi?"

"The last time I looked in on her she was sleeping. She wore herself out last night."

"Little wonder." He had already removed his hat and he raked his fingers through his wavy, uncombed hair as he paced the sitting room. "I wish I knew what to do next."

"Eat," Charity said sensibly. "You have to keep up your strength for whatever trials are to come. Seems to me you're the only member of your family capable of making wise decisions or taking any useful action."

"I'm afraid you're right, Miss Beal. Thank you for everything. I don't know what Naomi or Jacob would have done without you."

"You're most welcome."

Watching him leave the room she smiled knowingly. She hadn't expected Thorne to include himself in the gracious compliment but she could tell that he was as in need of her assistance as the rest of his party.

His self-confident nature wouldn't let him admit as much, of course, but she was content with knowing it was true.

The child in her lap stirred, blinked up through sleepy eyes and snuggled closer.

Charity hugged him to her and began to pray silently for his future. The way things looked now he was going to have a rough road ahead and she wished mightily that she could do more than merely comfort and care for him for the time being.

She laid her cheek against the top of his head and whispered, "He's yours, Father. Please bless and guide and watch over him."

A solitary tear slid from her eye and dropped onto the boy's hair. So young. *So innocent. Oh, dear God, help him.*

The ensuing days seemed to pass in a blur. Men of all kinds and all classes, including several of the hotel guests whom Thorne had originally deemed unfriendly, kept popping in to update him on the search. He had set up an office of sorts on the end of the counter behind which the desk clerk also stood so he could keep all the reports straight. It was his goal to speak personally with each and every searcher and thereby leave no stone unturned.

Upstairs, Naomi had taken to her bed and the doctor had diagnosed her condition as lingering hysteria. Thorne wasn't sure that was all there was to it. He'd seen plenty of people overcome by grief and disaster but he'd never known one to lapse into a state of near helplessness the way his sister-in-law had.

Thorne thanked God that Charity Beal had so readily assumed the role of his nephew's caretaker because he didn't know how he'd have adequately looked after everyone else and managed to coordinate a systematic search for Aaron at the same time.

A week had passed and they'd fallen into a routine that varied little from hour to hour, day to day. That was why Thorne was so astonished to suddenly see Naomi descending the stairs. She was dressed to go out and acting as if nothing unusual had happened.

Wearing her favorite traveling dress, a matching, ostrich-plumed hat and white lace, fingerless gloves, she carried only her reticule. Instead of approaching and greeting Thorne as he'd expected, she headed straight for the front door.

"Naomi!" he called. "Where are you going?"

She turned a blank stare toward him, said nothing, then continued out onto the boarded walkway.

As Thorne prepared to follow her he was detained by one of the regular hotel residents. He made short work of the tall, thin man's inane questions but by the time he reached the front door of the hotel, Naomi was already strolling away on another man's arm as if nothing was amiss.

Thorne raced after them and shouted, "Hey! Where do you think you're going?" He was nearly upon the pair before he recognized Naomi's beefy, reddish haired escort as one of the most recently arrived hotel guests.

The man paused and turned with a cynical expression. "The lady wanted to take a walk and I'm looking after her. What's wrong with that?"

"Nothing, under normal circumstances," Thorne replied. "But in this case I must insist we all return to the hotel. Immediately."

"No. I'm going home," Naomi said as if in a fog.

Thorne had touched her free arm to stop her from proceeding and was glaring at the other man when Charity joined them, toting Jacob on one hip.

The boy's enthusiastic squeal brought no visible reaction from his mother.

"What's the matter with her?" Charity asked Thorne.

"I don't know." He continued to gently restrain Naomi and she made no effort to escape. She also didn't seem to recognize her own son.

Ignoring the two men who appeared about to come to blows, Charity concentrated on Naomi and spoke gently. "Where are you going, dear?"

"To see my mama and papa." She sounded as if she, herself, were a child.

"Why don't we go inside and sit down to talk about it," Charity said. "You'd like to tell me about your trip, wouldn't you? I'd love to hear all about your parents. I know they're wonderful people. Aren't they missionaries to the Indians?"

"Yes," Naomi said. Her determination seemed to be wavering, so Thorne exerted a gentle pressure on her arm, guiding her away from the other man and back the way they'd all come.

Following, Charity whispered to Jacob. "Mama's still sick, dear. I know she loves you very much but she isn't herself right now."

In response, the confused child wrapped his pudgy arms around Charity's neck and laid his head on her shoulder. Her heart ached for him. In the space of a few brief days and nights she had grown to love the little darling as if he were her own and it pained her to see him so rejected and forlorn.

Leaving the portly, confused-looking man behind, Thorne led Naomi to the settee in the parlor where she perched primly on the edge of the velvet-covered cushions as if she were visiting strangers.

"I can't stay long," she said, removing her gloves and tucking them into her reticule. "Mama is waiting for me and she doesn't like it when I'm late for supper."

"Where is your mother?" Charity asked.

"Just up the road, I think." Naomi frowned momentarily. "I'm not really sure. I seem to be lost. But I know Mama will take care of me as soon as I can get home. She loves me, you know."

"I'm sure she does," Charity answered. Looking to Thorne she saw that he, too, was at a loss as to how best to respond.

"Why don't you stay a bit longer and have dinner with us," Charity said. "I'm sure your mama would want you to."

"Do you think so?"

"Yes, dear, I do. Mrs. Montgomery is roasting a brace of California quail that one of our guests brought us." She raised her head to sniff and added, "They smell delicious, don't they? And you must be famished."

Naomi nodded, still seeming befuddled. "Yes, I guess I am hungry. I don't know why I should be, though. Mama made me a wonderful breakfast this morning."

Eyeing Thorne to make sure he understood that she expected him to stay close by and observe, Charity said, "Actually, I need to go help in the kitchen and set the table. Would you two mind watching Jacob for me while I do that? He's a good little boy so I know you won't have any problems with him."

When Naomi didn't answer, Thorne held out his arms and took the child from Charity. "We'll be glad to, ma'am. Let us know if we can be of any other assistance."

Seeing the subdued two-year-old clinging to his uncle's neck while Thorne gently patted his back gave Charity a surprising pang of longing and blurred her vision enough that she turned and hurried away to hide her emotional reaction. That was what love should be like, she concluded. Simple and pure and safe, the way the child trusted that hardheaded yet tenderhearted man.

Too bad adult love couldn't be like that, she added, recalling her horrid marital experience. If she'd learned anything from her frightful days as Ramsey Tucker's wife it was that she wanted no part of the intimacy that marriage demanded. All she could recall of the few nights when he had accosted her was her own sobs and the way he had beaten her into silence. The only good thing about that was the oblivion of semiconsciousness that had spared her from feeling or hearing most of his disgusting advances.

Biting back tears, Charity busied herself by spreading a fresh linen cloth on the long, rectangular dining table and beginning to place the dishes and silverware. It had been a long time since she had questioned her current life or had entertained the slightest notion that there might be a different kind of happiness waiting for her just over the horizon. That notion was staggering. And frightening.

Rejecting it outright, she reminded herself that she was perfectly content to look after her dear papa and tend to the chores of the hotel. That was her lot in life and she was comfortable with it.

So why did she suddenly feel such a stirring of dissatisfaction? The Good Lord had rescued her from servitude to an evil, disreputable man and had reunited her with her loved ones. Why wasn't she the happiest woman in San Francisco—or in the whole country, for that matter?

"I am happy. And I love it here," she murmured.

Mrs. Montgomery chuckled from across the room as she used a corner of her apron to blot perspiration from her forehead. "I'm right glad to hear that," she said. "I don't know what I'd do without you, girl."

"You don't have to fret about that," Charity said.

"I'm never going to leave Papa. I promised him that long ago and I aim to keep my word."

Thorne held the child close and continued to stroke his back while Naomi prattled on about her life as a little girl. There was no doubt in Thorne's mind that his sister-in-law was a very sick woman. What he could hope to do about that without Aaron to help him was a different question.

The searchers had narrowed down the possibilities of Aaron's disappearance to one of two packet boats that had left the harbor with the mail soon after his abduction. That, or he had been spirited away overland, which was an unlikely scenario given the inherent difficulties in getting all the way back to New York via that route. Thorne had to assume that delivering Aaron to Louis was the kidnapper's assignment, else why take him at all?

No, Thorne had reasoned, they had to have left the city by sea. Since there was no use trying to catch up to the individual boats at this late date he had telegraphed ahead and already had dozens of men working on the puzzle. Until one of them wired back that he had located Aaron, there was nothing for Thorne to do but keep his vigil at the hotel.

He was relieved when Mrs. Montgomery summoned everyone for dinner. As soon as his gaze met Charity's he shook his head slightly in answer to her unspoken query.

She relieved Naomi of her hat, gloves and reticule,

then guided her to the same chair she had occupied the last time she and Aaron had eaten at that table, hoping it might trigger her memory. It didn't.

Thorne took a seat opposite his sister-in-law and gave Jacob the chair beside him, as usual. Many of the guests they had met during their stay had moved on. At present there was only Charity and her father, the proprietress and the young desk clerk, Thorne, Jacob, Naomi and two single men sharing the table. To Thorne's disgust, one of them resembled the fool who had tried to take Naomi out for a stroll and the other was the prattling idiot who had delayed him so long that she had almost escaped.

Thorne tried to make polite conversation with Charity while tolerating the other men for the sake of propriety. He was running out of things to say when a gangly, hatless youth with black elastic bands holding up his shirtsleeves burst into the hotel. His boots clomped on the wooden floor as he made straight for the dining room.

"Mr. Blackwell. I'm plumb glad I found you," he said, panting and looking extremely agitated.

Thorne's breath caught when he recognized the telegrapher. He pushed back his chair and stood. "What is it? Do you have news?"

"Yes, sir." The younger man handed him a slip of paper.

Reading it, Thorne tried to hide his distress. One quick glance at Charity's concerned expression told him he had failed.

She arose and circled her chair to join him. Gently laying her hand on his coat sleeve she urged him to share the message. "What have you learned?"

"They're absolutely certain that they traced Aaron and two other men to the port of Los Angeles, where they all boarded a ship bound for New York, as I had suspected they might."

"Then that's good news, isn't it?"

He shook his head. His heart was pounding and the hand that held the paper was trembling. "No. Not if he actually was aboard the *El Dorado*, as they believe. That ship just sank in a hurricane off the coast of Mexico with all hands reported lost."

Feeling Charity's fingers tighten on his forearm and seeing the compassion in her blue eyes, he covered her hand with his before he said, "It appears Jacob has no one left to look after him and his mother but me."

"What are you going to do?" Charity asked softly.

"I don't know."

From across the table, Naomi spoke as if she hadn't understood a thing they'd just said. "I must be going home to *my* mama soon. She'll be worried."

Thorne's gaze traveled from Naomi to Charity and then to the wide-eyed child. "You're right. You should go to your mother. We'll pack tonight and leave as soon as I can book passage on a packet boat headed north toward Puget Sound."

His fingers closed around Charity's. "I know this is sudden, Miss Beal, but will you come with us?

Jacob needs care and Naomi should have a gentle-woman like you as a traveling companion."

She pulled away. "I'm sorry. I can't."

"Why not? I'll pay you well for your trouble and treat you as if you were part of my family. I know it may be an arduous journey but surely, if you won't do it for Naomi, you'll take pity on the child."

"That's not fair," Charity said. "You know I care for him but my papa needs me and I promised I'd never leave him. I assure you, I take that vow quite seriously."

Emory cleared his throat, drawing everyone's attention. "I suspect this is a good time to make an announcement that I've been savin' for just the right moment." He reached for Annabelle Montgomery's hand and clasped it for all to see. "Mrs. Montgomery has consented to become my wife."

"Papa!" Charity was thunderstruck.

"Don't look so shocked, girl."

"But, what about Mama?"

He sobered and shook his head. "Your mama's gone to Glory but I'm still down here. And I'm not dead yet."

"I know, but…"

Emory was adamant as he beamed at his intended bride. "This is a fine, upstanding, Christian widow woman and I'm proud she fancies me. She'll make you a wonderful stepmother." He kissed his future wife's hand before he continued, "I release you from whatever promise you think you made, Charity, even though I don't recall any such nonsense. Your sister would already be upstairs packin' her duds if somebody had offered her an adventure like that. What're you waitin' for?"

Thorne could see that Charity was deeply hurt. He reached for her hand once again, hoping she wouldn't pull away. "Please? At least promise me you'll consider my offer?"

When she nodded, then turned and fled up the stairs to hide her tears, his heartfelt sympathy went with her. He knew *exactly* how it hurt to be treated as an outsider in one's own family. He'd dealt with that kind of unfair pain all his life. And he wasn't done doing so.

The two so-called gentlemen who had shared the communal meal in the Montgomery hotel stood in the shadows outside and spoke in whispers while they lit up after-dinner cigars. "Do you think it's true? Could the others all be dead?" the taller, thinner one asked.

His balding, stocky companion shrugged. "I don't know. Blackwell looked pretty upset when he heard the bad news but the wife didn't make a peep. It might be a ruse to throw us off the trail."

"And it might not. Now that there's maybe only two of us left, what do you think we should do?"

"Split up," the second man said, hooking a thumb in his vest pocket and leaning his head back to blow a succession of smoke rings. "You go back East by sea, explain this new development and tell the old man what we know so far."

"I don't much cotton to that idea. He's gonna be fightin' mad if it's true."

"Still, he's paid us plenty. He has to be informed, even if the news is bad."

"Oh, sure. And what're you gonna be doin' while he takes it out on me for bein' the messenger?"

"Getting even for our lost friends. Ashton's wife trusts me now. I'll stay close to her and her kin, wherever they go, and finish what we came for, one way or another."

"You sure you don't need my help?"

He shook his head, his thick jowls jiggling. "No. I can handle it. Even if I don't get another chance till they're on the trail, it'll be fine. All I'll have to do then is hang back and pick them off one at a time, starting with the brat."

The taller man winced. "I never did like that part of the job. Doesn't seem fair to kill him when we could just snatch him and maybe sell him, instead."

"That kind of thinking is clear stupid. Which is why I'm sending you home and handling things here by myself. When you talk to our boss, make sure you tell him straight out that I'm the one with the stomach for this job or you'll have to answer to me when I get back."

"*If* you get back."

His laugh was derisive. "Oh, I'll be back. And I'll expect to find a big bonus waiting for me when I show up in New York with the proof that I was successful."

"Proof? How're you gonna do that?"

The laugh deepened and took on a more sinister tone. "Same way the Indians do. I'll bring Ashton their scalps."

Chapter Four

Charity didn't know what to do. On the one hand she wanted to stay safely at home in San Francisco with her beloved papa. On the other hand, he had as much as told her she was no longer needed or wanted.

And what about poor little Jacob? He did need her and she did care about him. Why, oh why, did life have to be so complicated?

Standing in the middle of her sparsely furnished room she pivoted slowly as she took in the accommodations. There was a bed with a feather mattress atop tightly stretched ropes, a dressing table and mirror, a washstand with a pitcher and ewer, a small trunk containing most of her clothing, and pegs on the wall next to it where she could hang her few dresses and petticoats. The place wasn't lavish by any stretch of the imagination, yet it suited her. She didn't need much, nor did she deserve luxuries, although she had once thought otherwise.

Looking back, it was painful to envision how spoiled and selfish she had once been, not to mention the difficulties she'd caused her long-suffering sister, Faith, while they were crossing the prairie together.

Charity shivered and wrapped her arms around herself. Would she never be able to banish those horrible memories?

In the past, she had clung to them as if their presence was necessary to keep her humble. Now that she was being offered a chance to do something extraordinary for the benefit of an innocent child, perhaps that would be enough to cleanse her soul and give her the peace she had lost.

Verbal prayer was impossible with her mind whirling and her heart so torn and broken, but her unspoken thoughts reached out to God just the same. Was this what He wanted her to do? Was He giving her the second chance she'd so often prayed for? Or was she about to listen to her own confused feelings and become a victim of emotion and foolishness once again?

She pressed her fingertips to her lips and sank onto the edge of her bed. The tears she had begun to shed when her father had announced his forthcoming marriage were gone, leaving only a sense of emptiness. Of loss. Everyone she loved had left her; first Mama when the tornado had taken her life, then Faith when she'd married Connell and now Papa. It wasn't fair. She had given them as much devotion as she could muster, yet they were all gone now. Even Papa.

Bereft, she tilted her head back, closed her eyes and spoke to her Heavenly Father from the depths of her soul. "Please, tell me what to do? Please?"

She felt a soft tug on her skirt and opened her eyes. There at her feet stood the little boy whose well-being was at the heart of her concerns. She blinked. Smiled. Opened her arms, leaned forward and embraced him.

As she lifted Jacob onto her lap she sensed another presence and glanced toward the open door. Thorne was watching, silent and grave, clearly expecting her to speak.

Charity cleared her throat and smiled slightly before she said, "You really know how to influence me, don't you?"

"I hope so. Will you come with us?"

Sighing, she nodded and did the only thing that seemed right. She capitulated. "Yes."

Thorne was astonished that the slightly built young woman had agreed so easily. Now that she had, he was having second thoughts. Was he doing the right thing by including her in their traveling party? He knew having a female companion was best for Naomi and the boy but he wondered how much more trouble it was going to be looking after an extra woman, especially if the journey was as arduous as he feared it might be.

Then again, anyone who had crossed the great plains in a wagon and was now tolerating the constant earth tremors in San Francisco had to be made of sterner stuff than the average person. He didn't think he'd ever get used to all the shaking in that city, although its citizens seemed to take it in stride.

He huffed as he turned and headed back downstairs. They'd be safe enough in a hotel this substantial unless another big shake started more fires like the ones the citizenry had experienced several years back. Volunteer fire companies had been organized to handle small blazes but it was easy for fires in multiple locations to get away from them no matter how often they trained or how diligently they worked to douse the flames.

Once the city water system was completed that would help. So would rebuilding in brick as many had lately, he told himself, but there was still plenty of flammable material around, especially in the poorer sections of town.

Suddenly uneasy, Thorne paused at the base of the stairs and stood stock-still, his hand on the newel post. It hadn't been his imagination. The ground was trembling. Again. He could tolerate the pitching of a ship's deck in a storm at sea much easier than he could the unsteady shore. At least on board his ships he could predict oncoming swells and brace to ride them out. Here on land the shaking always took him by surprise.

He was still standing at the base of the stairs, waiting for further tremors, when Charity joined him.

He glanced past her. "Where's Jacob?"

"He fell asleep on my bed so I covered him, shut the door and left him there. He's exhausted, as well you can imagine."

"We all are," Thorne said with a sigh. "I must apologize for putting you in such an untenable position. If you don't wish to accompany my party, you don't have to."

"Yes, I do," she replied. "I knew that as soon as I looked into that poor little boy's eyes."

"You're very kind."

"No, I'm not. I have a lot of mistakes to make up for and helping you fulfill your obligation to your brother will start to pay that debt."

"I can't imagine what you could possibly have done that would call for such penance."

"It's not only what I did, it's what I didn't do when my sister needed me. It's only by the grace of God that she survived and we were reunited."

"Then you and I have even more in common than I thought," Thorne said with empathy. "I have often wondered why God continually spared my life during my years at sea."

"Really? Perhaps we were destined to work together for the common good."

His eyebrows arched. "Perhaps."

"Where's Naomi?" Charity asked. "Not gone off again, I hope."

"No. Mrs. Montgomery and your father are looking after her for the present."

"Good." Charity stepped down and led the way

to the parlor as she continued to speak. "My life began on a small farm in Trumbull County, Ohio. I thought I understood what hard work and deprivation were but until I crossed the prairie in a wagon train I had no true picture. That was the worst experience I have ever had."

Thorne stood until she had seated herself on the settee, then chose a nearby armchair. "Then you shouldn't go with us to the territories. It will be much more primitive up there than it is here."

"It wasn't the lack of amenities that bothered me. It was being married to evil personified, himself."

"You were *married?*"

"Yes. I thought my father had told you."

Thorne hoped he was successfully hiding his initial shock. "No. All he said was that you had undergone some terrible experiences during your journey. He never mentioned marriage."

"Hmm. I see." Lacing her fingers together in her lap, she paused for a moment before she went on. "I suppose you should know more particulars about my past before you actually hire me."

"That's not necessary."

"I think it is," she said, stiffening her spine, raising her chin and staring at the opposite side of the room as if she were gazing into the past. "I was very young. Just sixteen. We were halfway to California when my sister, Faith, was kidnapped by men we thought were Indians. I feared I'd never see her again."

"I'm so sorry."

"Oh, there's more," she said with resignation as her eyes met Thorne's. "I didn't know it at the time but the wagon boss, Ramsey Tucker, was not only responsible for Faith's disappearance, he got rid of her because he had designs on my father's gold-mining claim and she was too smart for him. She saw his true character while I was blind to it."

Thorne waited patiently for her to continue, aware that she was struggling to find the proper words and assuming she was trying to explain without exceeding the bounds of propriety.

Finally, Charity said, "Without my sister I was all alone, single and unescorted, and therefore in a terrible predicament, as you can imagine. I was so overwrought and afraid that I took the easy way out. I misjudged that horrid man and let him talk me into marrying him in order to continue the journey and find Papa again."

"Are you still married?" Thorne asked quietly.

Charity's eyes widened. "No! Nor was I legally wed in the first place, as it turned out, which makes everything even worse. Before he was killed, my so-called husband confessed that he was already married and had therefore led me, and countless other women, astray for his own disreputable gains."

She lowered her gaze to her clasped hands and Thorne noted that her knuckles were white from the pressure of her tight grasp.

"Surely, none of that was your fault," he said kindly.

"Wasn't it? I try to think about those awful days

as little as possible. No one here knows much about my past. Not even Mrs. Montgomery."

"Yet you just told me. Why?"

"Because I could be considered a loose woman, especially if we were to encounter any of the other folks who crossed the plains on the same wagon train or were present in the gold camp when my…husband… was killed."

Thorne had to smile. He leaned forward and rested his elbows on his knees, clasping his own hands. "Perhaps it will help if you know how I came to be called Blackwell while my brother is an Ashton."

"That isn't necessary," Charity said.

"Still, I think hearing this will make you feel less alone and help you understand why we all fear and loathe my stepfather the way we do. My mother began married life as Pearl Blackwell, then…"

As he concluded an abbreviated version his mother's tale he noted the concern in Charity's blue eyes. "Do you think Louis Ashton actually got rid of your real father so he could marry your mother, the way King David did to Uriah the Hittite in the Bible?"

"That was the way Mother told the story. She has come to that conclusion by piecing together the facts over the course of many years. As you did with your husband, she misjudged the kind of man Louis Ashton was and has been paying for her mistake ever since."

"Oh, poor Pearl. Can't you free her somehow?"

"Not as long as she chooses to remain in his house as Louis's wife. I've offered to support her for the rest of her days if she will leave him but she always tells me she considers her marriage vows sacred and won't break them. Not even now."

"How awful." Charity paled. "I suppose I should be more thankful that Ramsey Tucker is dead and gone."

"We have no control over things like that," Thorne said with resignation. "At least we shouldn't. For your sake, I'm glad he's no longer around to menace you."

To Thorne's relief he saw a slight smile beginning to lift the corners of Charity's lips.

"*Menace* is the *perfect* word to describe that man's behavior," she said. "I wasn't joking a bit when I referred to him as evil personified."

"I think I prefer to reserve that term for my stepfather."

"There really are a lot of evil people in this world, aren't there?"

"Yes. But you've been delivered from one of them and now it's time for the two of us to rescue Naomi and Jacob from another. Are you up to it?"

"Oh, yes," Charity said. "I'll be packed and ready to travel as soon as you say the word."

"You're sure? You're not afraid?"

She laughed lightly, her pink cheeks revealing a touch of embarrassment. "What does fear have to do with making this trip? As long as I believe—and I certainly do—that the Good Lord wants me to help you, why would I hesitate just because I happen to be scared witless?"

Thorne stood. "Good for you, Miss Beal. Forgive me for being so bold but I think you are one of the strongest, most worthy women I have ever had the pleasure to know."

"Let's hope your opinion has not changed by the time we reach Naomi's parents."

Nodding and politely taking his leave, Thorne kept his negative thoughts to himself. He was familiar with the upcoming sea voyage as far as the part of Poverty Bay now called Puget Sound. He'd even been to Admiralty Inlet, north of there, but that was as far as he'd traveled. Once they left the coast and started inland he'd be as lost as a sailor adrift in a lifeboat without compass or sextant.

Was this a fool's errand? he wondered. Perhaps. But he knew he must undertake it all the same. Even if his brother had not survived the sinking of the *El Dorado* there was still danger looming over Naomi and little Jacob.

Thorne could not, would not, abandon them to Louis's perfidy.

Pearl Ashton, red-eyed and clutching a lace-edged handkerchief, heard her husband opening the front door of their uptown mansion. She had been pacing the foyer and waiting for what seemed like hours.

Although her earlier tears had dried, the sight of Louis, so pompous and so handsomely clad in a gray cutaway coat, perfectly tailored pants and embroidered pearl satin vest brought fresh moisture to her eyes.

She dabbed the sparse tears away as she hurried toward him, the train from her bustle silently brushing the polished marble floor. "Where have you been?"

"I told you we were having another meeting of the Merchants' Society about that greensward we've been planning. We're going to call it Central Park if I have my way, and I believe I shall."

He scowled and peered past her as he removed his hat. "What is the matter with you, woman? And where in blazes are all the servants?"

"I sent them away."

Louis slapped his kid gloves into his overturned bowler. "What? Why on earth did you do that? I don't pay them to lollygag, you know."

"I wanted to be alone with you when I showed you this," Pearl said, reaching into the pocket of her skirt and producing a crumpled piece of yellow paper. Her hand was shaking as she thrust it at Louis.

Instead of accepting the paper, he strode past her toward the parlor as if she were far less important than the absent servants. "Just tell me what it says and be done with it, woman. I don't have time for your childish games."

"Childish?" Pearl's voice was strident enough that her husband hesitated. She knew she was already overstepping the limits of his volatile temper but at that moment she didn't care. She waved the paper. "What have you done?"

"I have no idea what you mean."

"No, of course you don't," Pearl said, nearly screaming at him. "First you drive away my eldest son and now this! How can you be so cruel?"

"What are you babbling about?" Louis grabbed the yellow telegram from her. As he scanned it, Pearl saw the color rise in his bearded cheeks.

"Is it true?" she demanded.

"What if it is? It's certainly no concern of yours."

"You've killed him!" she wailed. "You've killed my baby!"

"Don't be ridiculous. You're getting hysterical for no reason. All this says is that Aaron and some of my acquaintances are on their way back from Los Angeles."

"On the *El Dorado*." Pearl was sobbing as she raced to her favorite chair near the hearth, grabbed up the *New York Gazette* and returned to shove it in her husband's face. "Look, Louis. See for yourself."

She watched as the high color left him. He staggered back against the divan, his face pasty, his usually hawklike eyes growing rheumy.

"It sank!" Pearl screeched, beginning to beat on his chest and shoulders with her fists. "You couldn't let him go and now he's dead. I hate you. I hate you, do you hear? Of all the things you've done to ruin my life, this is the worst."

Louis regained enough self-control to grab her

thin wrists and stop her assault. "What do you mean, all the things I've done? What have I done except give you a life of luxury and treat you like a queen."

"A queen in a dungeon," Pearl countered. "You've deprived me of the love of both my sons."

"I've lost, too," Louis reminded her, thrusting her aside. "I loved Aaron as much as you did."

"But not Thorne. Never Thorne."

"Of course not. He wasn't my son."

Pearl crumpled on the velvet cushions of the divan and sobbed uncontrollably. Her heart was so badly broken she no longer feared for her own safety. If Louis chose to beat her for her outburst, or for what she was about to add, she believed she would welcome the pain, the eventual oblivion. Without her dear boys, life was not worth living.

After a few moments, sniffling and wiping her eyes, she got to her feet and faced the man to whom she had pledged her troth so many years before. As soon as he looked at her she demanded, "Tell me. How did you kill my beloved Samuel? Did you do it yourself or did you hire it done?"

Louis's eyes narrowed. "Don't be ridiculous. Samuel Blackwell was hit by a runaway dray after the driver lost control of his team. It was an accident."

"Was it?" Her chin jutted out, her lips pressed into a thin line. "Can you prove it?"

"Of course not. No more than you can prove it wasn't. There is something I *can* do, however. I can check with my friend James Bennett at the *Herald* instead of taking the word of the *Gazette*. If Bennett says he got the same news about the *El Dorado*'s sinking then I'll send men to Mexico to investigate and make certain the reports are accurate."

Pearl clasped her damp handkerchief in both hands and drew them to her chest over her cameo brooch. "Do you think they might be wrong? Could Aaron be alive after all?"

"If he is, I'll find him," Louis vowed. "And if you want to learn whatever facts I do manage to garner, I suggest you get control of your wild imagination and go back to being the well-behaved wife I expect you to be."

He had her. Pearl knew she would capitulate, as had always been her practice, and Louis would win again.

Drawing a hesitant, shaky breath, the enraged matron gritted her teeth and let her already-reeling mind spin out of control. If, in the final analysis, Aaron was really gone forever, perhaps she would join him in heaven. But, she added with surprising malice, she was not going to give up until she had sent Louis to a place where neither she, nor her loved ones, would ever have to see him again.

The cruelty and callousness of her malevolent thoughts shook her to the core. Had her trying years with Louis made her so hard-hearted that she could actually contemplate taking his life? Apparently so.

Weeping, she cried out to God for forgiveness, fell to her knees and begged Him for a return of the hope she had lost.

Chapter Five

Thorne spent the next morning at the docks, arranging passage for his party on the U.S. Mail Packet the *Grand Republic*. She wasn't big but she was a fast side-wheeler with a shallow draft and could therefore put them ashore almost anywhere along the coast if need be, an important advantage as far as Thorne was concerned.

There were plenty of other small packet boats he could have chosen. Steaming up and down the Pacific Coast, hauling mail, freight, passengers and gold dust had become a very lucrative business, especially in the five years since the original discovery of gold on the American River.

Once every fortnight, around the first and fifteenth of the month, larger freighters arrived in San Francisco Bay bringing supplies, as well as the latest news. Representatives of the city's twelve local papers waited at the docks for those dispatches, determined to be the first to disseminate information that may have come all the way from New York City, once the nation's capitol and still an important focal point of world affairs.

Thorne remained at the wharf in the hopes of getting his hands on further news about the ill-fated ship his brother had been aboard. He finally managed to obtain a newly arrived, abbreviated copy of the *New York Herald* and found the article he sought near the bottom of the second page.

It read:

The honorable Aaron Ashton, son of our fair city's esteemed banker, Mr. Louis P. Ashton, was reported to be a passenger aboard the three-masted freighter *El Dorado* when she floundered and sank in a frightful gale off the southern coast of Mexico last month. Local reports indicate that all unfortunate souls aboard were lost. Mr. Louis Ashton, a friend of the *Herald,* has indicated to us that he will sail for Mexico at the first opportunity to ascertain his son's whereabouts and to see to arrangements, if necessary. Our condolences and heartfelt prayers go out to the Ashton family.

Thorne crumpled the paper and threw it into the bay. He watched while the ebbing tide beat the few thin pages against the side of the wooden-hulled freighter until the paper disintegrated. Soaring, screeching gulls dived at the shreds as if they were as incensed and anxious as Thorne.

So, the old man was headed for Mexico, was he? Well, good. At least that quest would keep him busy and out of Thorne's hair for the present. If Aaron had managed to survive after all, Louis would see that he received the best care possible.

And in the meantime? Thorne turned and strode purposefully back toward the Montgomery House Hotel. In the meantime he would prepare his party as best he could and make ready to depart.

He would have preferred that no one else knew where he was bound or with whom. Unfortunately those plans were already common knowledge, thanks to his public discussion with Miss Beal at the hotel dinner table. He would, however, request that her father and Mrs. Montgomery keep their counsel if other seekers came later. Even with Aaron and his abductors out of the picture it was possible that Louis might send more villains to wreak havoc on what was left of his brother's family.

Instead of going to his room, Thorne went looking for Charity and found her in the kitchen, peeling potatoes for the large, afternoon meal.

"Forgive me for interrupting," he said with a polite nod as he removed his hat. "I wanted you to know I've arranged passage on the *Grand Republic*. We leave tomorrow morning on the outgoing tide."

Charity laid aside her paring knife and dried her

hands on her apron. Jacob, who was lurking in the folds of her skirt, giggled and ducked back to hide.

"You're going, too, little man," Charity said. "Won't it be fun! Your mama and Uncle Thorne and I are all going on a wonderful trip with you. We're going to see your grandma and grandpa White, up in Oregon."

"Papa?" the child asked.

"I expect your papa will join us as soon as he's able," she said.

Thorne assumed by her ensuing look of contrition that she was hoping the Good Lord would forgive her attempts to pacify the child by stretching the truth. He smiled benevolently at both her and Jacob, then met her gaze directly and merely said, "Thank you."

"You're quite welcome. I've laundered all of Jacob's things, except what he's wearing, and have done the best I could for Naomi, as well. We'll all be ready to go whenever you give the word."

Thorne reached into his pants pocket, withdrew a twenty-dollar Liberty Head gold piece, and handed it to her. "I should have been as considerate of your needs. Please consider this an advance on your wages and buy whatever you may need for yourself, Miss Beal. I want you to travel comfortably."

Seeming reluctant but smiling nevertheless, Charity accepted the coin and slipped it into her apron pocket. "I don't require much beyond what I already possess but I am obliged. Have you thought about other supplies we might need once we reach land again?"

"I figured to provision our party in Oregon or Washington Territories rather than try to buy everything here and transport it all that way. Since we don't know exactly what we'll face, it makes more sense to wait."

"I suppose so. But it will be much more expensive. My sister, Faith, and I paid dearly to stock up on flour and bacon in Fort Laramie."

"I'm sure you did. One added advantage we'll have is that the Northern Pacific railroad line has recently been completed as far as Puget Sound. Between that supply line on one side and the sea on the other, merchants should be well stocked."

"My, my. That's amazing. I had no idea."

Thorne saw her glance past him and pause. He looked over his shoulder and his curiosity turned to annoyance when he saw who was standing in the doorway. "Can we help you?" he asked the all-too-familiar, portly hotel guest.

The man smiled and nodded. "I couldn't help overhearin' you talkin' about headin' north. I have business in the territories myself and I was a mite curious, that's all."

"Then I suggest you get yourself down to the docks and find passage on a packet boat. There are plenty to choose from," Thorne said flatly. His stare was plainly meant to intimidate and the other man responded as he had hoped he would—he took his leave.

Thorne gave him plenty of time to have reached the front door, then spoke quietly to Charity. "Was he standing there eavesdropping for very long?"

"I don't know. I can't be certain. Why?"

"I don't like him."

"That's probably because he took Naomi for a walk without your permission. He seems harmless enough to me, pretty full of himself but otherwise not particularly odious."

"When did he first come here? Do you remember?"

"A few days ago. I can check the register if you want me to be more precise. I think his name starts with an S. Maybe it's Smith." She chuckled demurely. "Like yours."

"Very funny. I suppose there must be some genuine Smiths somewhere or it wouldn't be such a common name."

"I suppose so."

Thorne had run out of valid reasons to linger in the kitchen. He reached into his pocket and withdrew a large key, gesturing with it as he said, "I'll go check on Naomi. I trust she was well this morning?"

"As well as can be expected." Charity gently stroked Jacob's hair as she spoke. "Mrs. Montgomery has been brewing motherwort tea for her three times a day, with a touch of lady slipper root and ginger. That seems to be helping settle her nerves. We haven't heard her pounding on the door or raising a ruckus at all lately."

"Good. I've asked the doctor for a bottle of laudanum, too, in case she becomes more unhinged while we're traveling."

"Do you really think that's necessary?"

"I hope not," Thorne said soberly. "I sincerely hope not."

Charity had grown more and more agitated as the day had progressed. She doubted she'd sleep a wink all night, especially since she was now sharing her narrow bed with the wiggly child.

That situation couldn't be helped, she reasoned, gazing fondly at the place atop her mattress where Jacob lay, already napping. Poor little man. He was exhausted, as well he should be, given his trying circumstances.

She had often tried to return him to his mother during the past three or four weeks. Each time, Naomi's unbalanced mind had demonstrated how unwise that would be. Since Jacob's mother had no idea who he was, there was no way Charity was going to leave them alone together. For all she knew, Naomi didn't even remember how to properly care for a young child.

She took a deep breath and released it as a sigh. Looking at her meager pile of belongings she was struck by how cumbersome the small trunk would be, especially if they were forced to travel astride horses or mules instead of employing a wagon on the final leg of their journey. Perhaps Mrs. Montgomery had a large carpetbag she could borrow. If not, she'd ask her to watch over Jacob in case he awoke and she'd make a quick trip to the dry goods store at the corner of Dupont and Washington.

Charity glanced out the window of her second-story room and hoped she hadn't waited too long to make this decision. Dusk was nearly upon the city, the rays of the setting sun reflecting off the waters of the bay and the ocean beyond to bathe the buildings in warm color.

In that muted, golden light it was easy to overlook the muddy streets and the unattractiveness of the poorer sections of town, especially those nearest the wharf. Washington Street was due to be paved in stone soon, from Dupont to Kearney, so Charity knew it was only a short time before those buildings bordering it would also be spruced up. The canvas and tar paper shacks of the gold-rush era were quickly being replaced with real buildings, thanks in part to the new law forbidding frame structures within the densely built sections of the city, and she was often awed by the rapid changes.

Hurrying downstairs, she found Mrs. Montgomery in the parlor, knitting while visiting with Emory. It was still hard for Charity to picture that woman taking her mother's place but she couldn't fault her father for being lonely. She just wished they could all go back to being the close family they had been when she was a girl—before he had headed for California to seek his fortune.

The happy couple were chatting away as if they were the only two people in the world and Charity was struck by the notion that maybe her father had found true riches, after all. He had definitely found another life's mate. Although she was glad for him, she was also quite aware that she was the only member of her family who was still alone, still unsettled.

Forcing a smile she entered the parlor and greeted her future stepmother. "Annabelle, I wonder if you might have a carpetbag I could use? I've decided it will be too much of a bother to tote my trunk."

The older woman returned her smile. "I'm sorry, dear, I don't. You can probably get one at the mercantile."

"I know. That was my second choice. Could you keep an eye on Jacob for me while I run down there? He shouldn't be any bother. He's sound asleep on my bed and I shut the door so outside noises won't wake him."

"Of course. Don't you worry one minute. I'll run up and check on him right soon."

"There's no hurry," Charity said, wrapping a shawl around her shoulders and wishing she'd thought to fetch a bonnet before she'd left her room. Well, that couldn't be helped. If she was going to reach the store before the clerks locked up for the night she'd have to go without one.

"I'll be back in two shakes of a lamb's tail," she called over her shoulder as she headed for the front door.

The heels of her dainty shoes tapped on the boards of the raised walkway, reminding her that it would be a good idea to purchase a sturdy pair of boots, as well as the carpetbag. It hadn't been that long ago that she'd struggled to cross the barren plains and there had been many times during that trek when she had wished mightily for more substantial footwear.

She was almost running when she reached the corner where the dry goods store stood. The shade was pulled and the sign in the window read Closed.

Breathless, she rapped on the glass window in the entrance door and called, "Hello? Are you still there?"

The face of a familiar gentleman appeared. He recognized her, unlocked the door and peered out.

"I'm sorry to call so late," she said. "But I'm sailing tomorrow and…"

He smiled graciously, stepped back and Charity darted inside.

Thorne had been in the What Cheer saloon, making plans to have some of the local men continue to watch for signs of his brother in spite of the probability that he would never return when he'd noticed a young woman in a yellow gingham dress hurrying past on the far side of the thoroughfare. He recognized Charity Beal immediately. Worried, he left his companions to follow her. When he reached the street, however, she was out of sight.

His thoughts immediately turned to Jacob and Naomi. Yes, he believed they would be safe at the hotel because there were so many others present, yet the fact that Charity was away gave him pause. He figured she was merely out seeking something else to take on their trip but that probably meant that there was no one specifically looking after the boy.

The hackles on the back of Thorne's neck prickled a warning. Concerned, he wheeled and headed back toward the hotel at a trot.

Annabelle had been having such a wonderful time making plans for the future with her groom, she waited longer than she had intended before going to check on the sleeping child. Climbing the stairs wasn't as easy for her at sixty as it had once been, nor was it painless. Every change in the weather brought new aches and the harder she labored, the more she hurt, which meant that going from the first to the second floor was neither easy nor enjoyable.

Still, she had promised Charity she'd look in on Jacob, so she would make the extra effort. She was halfway up when Thorne straight-armed the door behind her and strode into the lobby.

Annabelle paused and greeted him. "Oh, good. You're here so you can go check on the boy. I was goin' to but these old bones are achin', and that's a fact."

"He's alone?"

"Sleeping. Miss Charity put him to bed in her room and he hasn't made a peep. I've been listenin'."

Thorne hurried past. She was far enough up the stairway to watch the big man go directly to Charity's door and ease it open.

A few seconds later his shout startled her so badly she nearly lost her balance. Grasping the banister she struggled the rest of the way up and found him on his knees on the rag rug next to Charity's bed. He was hugging Jacob. The child was clinging to his neck and sobbing.

Concerned and winded, Annabelle leaned on the doorjamb for support. "What's wrong? Is he sick?"

The look Thorne shot her in reply was so alarming it made her demand more answers. "What's happened? Tell me."

"I don't know," Thorne said. "When I got here he was sitting on the floor, crying. All I've been able to get out of him was that he was going to see his papa."

"Maybe he was dreaming," the older woman suggested.

Thorne rose with the sobbing youngster in his arms. "I don't think so. He kept saying he wanted to go with the man."

"To—to see my papa," Jacob stuttered, sniffling.

"What man?" Annabelle asked. "Where is he?"

The boy pointed across the room. "Gone."

"Out the window?" Thorne asked.

Jacob nodded, his dark curls bobbing.

Rather than carry his precious burden to the window and expose him to possible lingering danger, Thorne handed him to Mrs. Montgomery. "Here. And don't let him out of your sight."

She stood there, holding the boy and staring, openmouthed, as Thorne lifted the sash as high as it would go, bent double and stepped out onto the roof of the porch below.

"Do you see anybody?" she called.

"No. I'm going to climb on up to check the rest of the roof. Take Jacob downstairs and stay with Emory until Charity gets back."

Not about to argue with such a forceful man, especially since he was so upset, the proprietress did as she was told.

She had just reached the parlor, carrying the sniffling child, when she heard a woman's piercing scream echo from the street outside.

Chapter Six

Returning to the hotel with her purchases, Charity wouldn't have noticed the two figures atop the hotel roof if a woman across the way hadn't shrieked and pointed.

Mindful of the horse-and-wagon traffic in the muddy street, Charity nevertheless left the raised walk and quickly maneuvered until she was in a position to view what was going on.

She froze, squinted and shaded her eyes. Was that who she thought it was? Was Thorne Blackwell actually scrambling along the rooftop, *chasing* someone?

Backlit by the setting sun, the two men appeared little more than shifting shadows, yet she instantly recognized Thorne from the way he moved, the shape of his broad shoulders, the cut of his clothes. It was him, all right, and he was gaining on his agile, more slightly built quarry.

Thorne lunged. He grabbed for the other man and managed to catch hold of his ankle. Both figures fell, and the slam of their bodies hitting the metal roof carried all the way to the street below.

As Charity watched, the thinner man used his free leg to kick at Thorne and caught him in the shoulder. Thorne lost his grip and went skidding toward the edge of the corrugated tin roof as if the surface were greased.

Charity was too stunned to remember to pray. She gasped and held her breath as Thorne rolled onto his back, dug in his heels and slowed his descent. He finally came to a halt mere inches from the edge of the precipice.

Instead of abandoning his pursuit the way Charity had expected him to, he immediately turned and started to climb back to the crest of the roof, moving like one of the hundreds of tiny crabs that crowded the shore at low tide.

As soon as he reached the highest peak, he braced himself and straightened, his hands on his hips. Charity assumed from his stillness that his target must have escaped.

She watched until he had given up, edged safely back down onto the porch roof and was preparing to enter one of the windows. That was when she realized that he was climbing into *her* room! The very room where she had left Jacob.

Frightened beyond imagination, Charity hiked her skirts and raced back across the rutted street toward the hotel. Not even stopping to wipe her feet, she dropped her purchases inside the door, crossed the lobby and bolted up the stairs just in time to confront Thorne as he exited her room.

"What is it?" she asked breathlessly. "Is Jacob all right?"

"Yes." He was scowling. "Why did you leave him alone?"

"I didn't. He was sleeping so I asked Mrs. Montgomery to look in on him while I ran to the store. I never have stayed with him every waking moment." She tried to squeeze past.

Thorne reached out and grasped her arm to stop her. "You're right. I'm sorry. I shouldn't have blamed you."

"For what, exactly? What's happened?"

"Someone tried to take him," he said flatly.

"What?" Frantic, she twisted to free herself. "Let me go. I have to see him."

"Settle down. He's safe now. He's with Mrs. Montgomery and your father."

"Oh, thank the Lord!" Charity said, meaning the praise with every ounce of her being.

Suddenly weak-kneed, she was glad Thorne had not yet released his hold on her. She sagged within his grasp. He stepped to her side to begin guiding her down the stairs toward the parlor.

"I saw you out on the roof just now," Charity said as they descended. "Was that man the one who tried to steal Jacob? Was that why you were chasing him?"

"Yes. Jacob told me he had fled out the window. When I followed, I spotted him running away."

"Did you recognize him?"

"I'm not sure. I think he may have been one of the hotel guests."

"The man who was listening to us talk in the kitchen?" she asked, barely whispering and looking from side to side to make certain they were alone.

"No. A different person. I don't recall his name but I'm fairly certain I've seen him around." His frown deepened and he paused with her before they reached the ground floor. "As a matter of fact, I think he's one of the volunteers who was helping me search for Aaron."

"But, why would he try to take Jacob?"

"Probably because he's working for my stepfather," Thorne said with obvious malice.

His arm tightened around her shoulders and Charity permitted the social faux pas. At that moment she needed Thorne's strong moral and physical support more than she needed to maintain her usually prim demeanor. Jacob had been in mortal danger and she had failed him. She could only thank a benevolent providence for the child's deliverance.

That was a direct answer to her prayers for Jacob and Naomi's safety, she realized with a start. Even though she had temporarily failed in her duty, God had looked after the innocent little boy. *And his mother, also?* she asked herself.

Grasping the banister with her right hand, she

swiveled to look back up the stairs. "Wait. Have you checked on Naomi, too?"

Thorne froze. "That's where I was headed when I ran into you. Stay here."

"Not on your life," Charity said. "From now on, where you go, I go."

"No. It might be dangerous."

Charity gave a nervous laugh as she dogged his steps in spite of his sensible admonitions. "Fine," she muttered, speaking as much to herself as to Thorne, "if you get into any more trouble like you did on the roof, I'll be there to clunk the other fellow over the head and rescue you."

Naomi was asleep when Thorne unlocked her door but he thought it best to rouse her and make certain she was unmolested.

"Naomi?" He gently touched her shoulder.

"Oh. Is it morning?" she asked, yawning and blinking rapidly. "Dear me. I seem to have fallen asleep without getting ready for bed. What will Mama say?"

"I'm sure she won't be upset," Charity volunteered. "Are you feeling better after your nap?"

"Fit as a fiddle." The paler woman swung her feet over the side of the bed and looked at her own feet. "My, my, I've left my shoes on, too. How silly of me."

She stood, stretched, then smoothed her fitted jacket over her skirt with a delicate tug at the braid decorating the bottom edge, as well as the collar and cuffs. "Well, I'd best be going."

"I think you should come downstairs with us," Charity said before Thorne could object.

He agreed. "You're right. It will be best if we all stick together until we sail." Looking to Charity he added, "You can sleep with Naomi tonight and I'll keep the boy with me. We'll leave our door open so we'll hear you if you call out."

"Do you really think that's necessary?"

"Vital. Do you have a gun?"

"No. I've never been fond of firearms."

"Well, you'd better get fond of them because you may need to defend yourself. Have you ever learned to shoot?"

"Yes. Faith insisted I practice with Papa's old Colt. It was so heavy I had to use two hands to lift it."

"I'll find you something lighter, something you can safely carry in your apron pocket or your reticule."

"If you insist."

Seeing Charity shiver and pull her lacy shawl closer brought a tightness to his gut. What had he gotten her involved in? And how was he going to protect all three of his charges if they were ever separated? Jacob was dear to his heart and Naomi was kin, but the notion of having to choose them over Charity Beal gnawed at his conscience. The only sensible conclusion was to see that the four of them were together all the time until he had delivered Naomi to her parents. After that, he'd simply escort Charity back to San Francisco and everyone's troubles would be over.

Thorne would have felt a lot better about those logical conclusions if his heart and mind had not immediately countered them with serious misgivings. First, it would be improper for him to travel with only Charity. Although she was perfect as Naomi's chaperone and Jacob's caretaker, escorting a lovely, single woman like her posed an altogether different moral dilemma.

And that wasn't all that was bothering him. There were clearly forces of evil at work. Try as he might, he couldn't seem to clear his mind of vivid images of impending doom. Images that involved Charity Beal.

Naomi had taken Thorne's arm, leaving Charity to follow them down the stairs. She wasn't offended. After all, she reminded herself, she was merely the hired help, not a part of his family, no matter what he had promised about treating her as such. Besides, she had only accepted the position because she cared about poor little Jacob.

And now look what's happened, she chided. *You left him alone and he was nearly kidnapped. Or worse!*

That dire conclusion brought unshed tears to her eyes. She had made a bad mistake and the Lord had sent Thorne to set things right again. She would not make any more errors of judgment. From now on she was going to stick closer than that child's shadow. No one was going to harm him. Not while she still had breath in her body.

When they reached the lobby, Charity dodged past

the others and made a beeline for Annabelle and the boy. It was clear that Jacob had been crying because his eyes were red and his cheeks streaked by tears.

She held out her arms. He immediately scrambled down from Mrs. Montgomery's ample lap and ran to Charity as fast as his short, pudgy legs would carry him.

She scooped him up and held him tight for a long moment before she smiled and said, "Look at you. We need to wash your face."

"I want my papa," he whined.

"I know you do, dear. But I can't do anything about that right now." Balancing him on one hip she started toward the kitchen. "Let's go get you cleaned up and then maybe we can find you another cookie. How does that sound?"

A glance back toward Thorne told her he wasn't keen on having the child out of his sight for even a few minutes.

"We'll be right here in the kitchen," she said flatly. "If you want to join us, you're most welcome, but it's not necessary. I will not leave him alone again, I promise you. Not for any reason."

"We'll be right here, talking," Thorne said as he formally escorted Naomi to the settee and placed her beside Annabelle. "Don't be long."

"No longer than it takes to wash and find a treat." Charity smiled. "And don't bother telling me I'm spoiling him. I know I am. And I fully intend to continue."

To her relief, Thorne returned her smile, although

his was more lopsided and wry than what she was used to seeing. It gave him an impish air that she fancied was more a reflection of the boy he had once been than of the man he had become.

"I'm not at all surprised," he said. "I'd be doing the same thing if I were not otherwise occupied."

"Then I'll give him a cookie on your behalf, too. How does that sound?"

With his eyes glittering suspiciously and his voice hoarse he answered, "Please do."

Charity was so touched by the tenderness she noted in Thorne's response she had to bite her lip to keep from weeping tears of joy and relief. They had had a terrible scare, one that might very well have spelled the end of their proposed rescue mission, and she was so thankful to have the child in her arms, healthy and unharmed, that she would have given him just about anything he had asked for.

The one thing she couldn't give him, of course, was the return of his missing father. It was hard to believe Aaron was actually deceased, although all indications pointed to that heartrending result.

Then again, Charity told herself, the ways of the Lord truly were mysterious. Aaron could still be alive even if he had been shipwrecked.

Thinking that gave her an inkling of peace and she chose to latch on to the possibility that he had survived rather than dwell on his probable death.

She sat Jacob on the edge of the enameled sink while she pumped fresh water to wet a clean cloth.

"This is a bit cold," she said, wiping his cheeks, "but your face is really dirty, you know that?"

He nodded and accepted her ministrations stoically. "Uh-huh." Looking past her shoulder at the doorway into the parlor, he asked, "Is Uncle Thorne mad at me?"

"Oh, honey, no," Charity said quickly, kissing his damp forehead. "He was just worried, that's all. You must never go off with strangers, not even ones that seem nice or say they can take you to your papa. Promise?"

His lower lip quivered. "Uh-huh."

"Good." She tried to lift his spirits by pretending she wasn't concerned when what she really wanted to do was clasp the child tightly to her breast for the rest of the day and night. "Now, how about that cookie?"

"Two cookies," the bright child said as she lifted and set him on the floor. "One from you and one from Uncle Thorne."

Charity laughed. "That's right. Hold up your fingers and show me how many that is."

When he struggled to display only two fingers and finally succeeded, she clasped his hand and kissed his extended fingers. "That's right. What a smart boy you are."

"I'm almost three," Jacob said, laboriously adding another digit and displaying the count.

"That's wonderful. When is your birthday?"

He looked puzzled, then brightened. "Mama knows. We can ask her."

Charity had to turn away. She busied herself getting his cookies while she sought to compose herself. What were they going to do if Naomi never regained her memory or even came to her senses about the simplest things? What if she continued to believe that she, too, was a child? What would happen to her little boy then?

The dreadful consequences of such a misfortune were unthinkable.

"Hey, don't look at me like that. I almost had him," the wiry young man said.

"And nearly got yourself into serious trouble. I told you I'd take care of it."

"Yeah, yeah, I know. You just want all the glory for yourself."

"I deserve it," the heavier man replied, giving his tall companion a look of disdain. "I never would have tried a stunt like you pulled. Not right under their noses. What were you thinking, man? What if you'd gotten caught?"

"But I didn't." He peered from one end of the alleyway to the other, clearly wary and understandably nervous.

"Not yet you haven't. The night is still young." Blowing puffs from his cigar into rings, the heavyset smoker paused for effect before he said, "If I were you, I'd be down at the docks right now, looking for passage out of here on the first boat I could find, like I told you."

"I was goin' to do that come morning."

"No. You'll do it now. I don't want you hanging around here drawing attention to me." He patted his cuff where they both knew he carried a hidden derringer. "The way I see it you have a choice. Either you hightail it for the boats or I'll shoot you where you stand and eliminate any connections between us. It's up to you."

"Okay." He held up his hands in a gesture of compliance. "I'll go." Glancing toward the hotel windows above he added, "What about my clothes?"

"I'll pitch them out the window for you. If you or any sign of you is still in San Francisco in another hour, you're a dead man."

"We were partners," his companion grumbled. "Why should you want to kill me?"

"For sheer stupidity if nothing else. Now, stay put and keep out of sight. I'll go get your things."

"There's a pistol under my pillow. Don't forget that."

The stronger-willed assassin laughed coarsely. "You must think I'm a fool. You'll get it—but without any bullets."

"Awww… What'll happen to me if I ain't armed?"

His eyes narrowed menacingly. "One more word out of you and neither of us will have to worry about what happens to you, gun or no gun. Is that clear?"

"Yeah. I s'pose I can get more black powder, ball and caps down in Chinatown. Just hurry it up, will ya?" His wary gaze darted to the streets at either end of the alley as if expecting imminent attack.

"I'll be shoving your clothes out that window just as soon as I can sneak into your room." He pointed up with his half-smoked cigar. "Be ready."

"What if somebody sees you?"

"Then I'll play it safe, protect myself, and you'll be leaving without your duds. Just remember you're leaving, period. Even if it's feetfirst."

Chapter Seven

Charity packed everyone's clothes except Thorne's and turned in early that night. Naomi caused her no trouble, thanks to another cup of Mrs. Montgomery's special tea, but every creaky board, every quarrelsome gull that perched on the porch roof, every passing carriage or horseman below seemed to startle Charity and keep her from falling asleep. As a consequence, she was exhausted in the morning when Thorne rapped on the door to her room.

She gathered her wrapper around her and tied the sash on her way to the door. "Who is it?"

"It's me," he said. "We should leave within the hour."

Opening the door a crack Charity hid behind it and peeked out. "We'll be ready. Naomi is still sound asleep but I'll have her up and dressed in plenty of time. I promise."

"You look tired," he said gently.

"I am, and that's a fact." She peered past him and scowled. "Where's Jacob?"

"Downstairs with Mrs. Montgomery and your father." He began to smile. "You should see those two working together in the kitchen. She's giving the orders like a ship's captain and he's trying to keep up with her. Looks to me as if she'll be wanting to hire some more help very soon."

"I don't doubt that. Papa never was much of a cook or housekeeper. His miner's cabin at Beal's Bar was pretty rustic."

Loath to shut the door all the way and bid him goodbye, she tarried a moment longer. When Thorne took a step back she assumed she was keeping him. "I don't want to delay you. We'll be down in a jiffy."

It pleased her to see that Thorne seemed as reluctant to depart as she was to have him leave.

Finally, he asked, "Do you want me to wait out here until you're ready?"

"Mercy, no. By the time we dress and do our hair up properly you could be through eating breakfast."

Still, he hesitated. "I don't know that I should leave you."

"We'll be fine. This is a respectable hotel and one of our clerks is on duty all night. I warned him to be on the lookout for the man you caught bothering Jacob, so I know there's nothing to worry about."

Thorne nodded. "All right. I'll stop by the front desk and check with him about it just to be sure. In the meantime, you ladies make ready to travel. And be sure you have your heavy coats. It can get blustery on board those packet boats, even if they do stay closer to shore than my heavier freighters. You'll doubtless need warm clothing the farther north we sail, too."

"Oh, dear. I hadn't thought of that. I'm afraid I don't have anything really heavy."

"Then bring Aaron's overcoat for yourself," Thorne said. "I was planning to leave his suits and things behind for your father, anyway. Emory won't need that coat nearly as much as you will."

"All right. Perhaps I can take my sewing box and make the necessary alterations while we're traveling." She wasn't pleased when Thorne laughed.

"Do as you wish. Just remember, the less we have to transport, the easier the trip will be," he said.

"I know." Pursing her lips and making a face she nevertheless had to admit he was being sensible. "All right. I'll wear the coat as it is and roll up the sleeves if need be. Will that satisfy you?" Seeing his continuing amusement, she added, "What's so funny?"

"Nothing. I apologize. I was just picturing you floundering around in that big coat."

"I never flounder. Besides, if your brother's coat warms me when I would otherwise be freezing, I certainly won't let pride keep me from wearing it. Now, if you'll excuse me…"

She eased the door closed and left him standing there in the hallway, grinning like a child with his hand in a penny candy jar at the mercantile. She had been honest when she'd insisted she wasn't prideful. Now that she thought more about their upcoming situation she decided it was just as well she wouldn't look very appealing while clad in Aaron's oversize coat.

The last thing she wanted was to make herself attractive to a man—any man—and her burgeoning feelings for Thorne Blackwell and his nephew would be far better denied than expressed.

Yes, he already knew she cared deeply for the boy but that was simply a mother's instincts. All women had those. It was her undeniable affinity for Jacob's taciturn yet intriguing uncle that threatened to be her undoing.

Charity pressed her back against the closed door, looked around and sighed. This was the last time she would see this cozy room for who knew how long, and the thought of leaving San Francisco and all that was familiar tugged at her heart. She knew that sacrifice was necessary. She also knew she was doing the right thing.

Nevertheless, she wished she could change the current circumstances. The notion of making a journey into a wilderness that lay beyond her current experience was unsettling. The idea of doing so in the company of a forceful man like Thorne Blackwell was doubly so.

Thick, damp, bone-chilling fog shrouded the city as Thorne led his little party toward the wharf where the *Grand Republic* awaited. He knew the crew would already have a head of steam built up in preparation for sailing and he was in a hurry to board.

The docks were bustling with activity in spite of the dreariness of the early morning. Bulging cargo nets swung from overhead hoists mounted on the foredeck while dozens of men pushed heavily laden carts across rickety planks that spanned the short distance between the pier and the boat's portside. Over the years, many a hapless man had missed his footing and plunged to his death from such planks. It was a hazardous profession but never lacked for willing workers.

Thorne hired a man to follow with their luggage, then began to escort the adults in his party across the planks one at a time, beginning with Charity so he could safely pass Jacob into her care.

"Take him and wait right here with our bags while I get Naomi," he ordered.

Charity smiled and gave him a mock salute. "Yes, sir."

He understood that she was merely trying to lighten his mood but he couldn't bring himself to respond in kind. Maybe it was because of the foggy morning or maybe he was just unduly jumpy, but he couldn't seem to banish the sense that they were being watched.

His footsteps echoed hollowly on the springy plank as he returned to shore for his sister-in-law. She wasn't where he had left her! For an instant he feared that she had wandered off again. Then, he spotted her about fifteen feet away, standing with her back to the *Grand Republic*.

It wasn't until Thorne drew closer that he realized she was in the company of the same portly man who had tried to take her for a walk near the hotel.

He quickened his approach. "Hey, there. What do you think you're doing?"

The man doffed his hat to reveal thinning, reddish hair and smiled instead of retreating. "I was just telling this dear lady that I was certain you would be right back." He took a step to the side as Thorne grasped Naomi's arm. "I remembered how upset you were the last time we met so I refrained from allowing her to talk me into escorting her anywhere. I trust that suits your pleasure?"

"Yes." Thorne nodded, polite but wary. "Thank you."

Starting to guide Naomi away, he scowled at the other man. "What brings you to the docks so early? Did you find the passage you wanted?"

"I certainly did," the man said. He raised his lit cigar and blew a smoke ring that disappeared almost instantly in the pea soup air. "I'm sailing aboard this very boat. You?"

"We're on the *Grand Republic*, too."

"Excellent." He extended his hand. "Allow me to introduce myself. Cyrus Satterfield, recently of Philadelphia. I believe I had the pleasure of dining with you several times at the Montgomery House Hotel."

Although Thorne was hesitant, he responded out of habit and shook the other man's hand. "Smith," he said.

"And you're from…?"

"I live at sea," Thorne told him. "Excuse us."

"Of course, of course. I'm sure we'll have plenty of time to get better acquainted while on board."

Thorne had made up his mind long ago that he was going to keep his family from getting acquainted with any other travelers. Now that he knew Cyrus Satterfield was aboard, he was even more determined to sequester them. There was something about the man that bothered Thorne. He recalled that Charity hadn't had the same misgivings, yet he couldn't seem to banish his concern.

Perhaps Satterfield was simply an unctuous fool. Then again, perhaps Thorne's first impression had been the right one. He'd disliked the man from the moment he'd first laid eyes on him.

Charity tried to distract herself, and Jacob, by showing him all the interesting cargo that was piled on the open, lower deck of the steamboat. There was extra wood for the boilers, sack goods such as grain and milled flour, barrels of pickles, crackers and hardtack, enormous bales of what looked like fodder for the sheep penned on the foredeck, a few cages filled with hens and all sorts of other miscellaneous freight.

She smiled as Thorne and Naomi joined them. "Jacob likes these chickens. He wanted to know if he could have one as a pet."

"Maybe your grandma White has chickens where she lives," Thorne replied. He gestured with his free arm. "We should go on up to the passenger deck so we're not in the way while the longshoremen finish loading and the crew prepares to cast off."

Charity, toting Jacob on one hip, led the way. "Oof," she told the child, "you're getting heavy now that you're almost three years old. What a big boy you are."

"His birthday is in June," Naomi said. Then she flushed and looked astonished. "Mercy me. How do you suppose I knew that?"

Charity didn't know what to say in response so she remained silent.

"It's the tenth, if I remember right," Thorne volunteered. "We should be at his grandparents' by then. We'll have to have a birthday party."

"With cake," the child added, clearly delighted. "I like chocolate. Mama always makes it for me."

It tore at Charity's heart to see the little boy look at his mother so lovingly. It was evident he now expected her to begin talking to him the way she used to but the woman had resumed her blank stare. Whatever twist of fate had triggered her sudden recall, the occasion had apparently passed.

"Well, if your grandmother doesn't know how to bake the kind of cake you like, I do," Charity said. "I'll see that somebody makes you one for your birthday. Okay?"

He nodded so hard his curls bobbed. "Okay!" Wrapping his arms around her neck he added a soft, tender, "I love you."

If she hadn't been in such close proximity to the

rest of the family she would have buried her face in his curls and allowed herself to weep.

As it was, she simply gave him a hug, forced a smile and said, "I love you, too, sweetheart."

Thorne could tell that Charity was getting far too attached to the child for her own good. He knew exactly how that could happen. He'd done the same thing on their journey around the horn.

At his young age, Jacob was open and loving to a fault. He had not yet realized the extent of the disappointments that life had dealt him, nor would he have to bear them alone, if Thorne had his way. He didn't know how he was going to accomplish that, especially once they delivered Naomi and the boy to the missionaries, but he was certainly going to try. Above all, he was going to keep sending money for their support so they never became a financial liability to anyone.

Louis Ashton had always complained loudly about the terrible burden Thorne's presence had caused. One of the most violent outbursts had occurred shortly before Thorne had left home for good.

"I can do as I please whether you like it or not," Louis had shouted at his wife. "If I choose to beat the no-good boy within an inch of his life, it's my right."

"You have no rights to him," Pearl had sobbed as she'd clung to her husband's sleeve to stay his hand. "No rights!"

"I'm his father, remember? You should. It's your fault I was saddled with raising him."

"He goes by my first husband's name already. What more do you want?"

Louis had laughed maniacally then. "What I want is illegal, my dear, or I would have put him in the ground when he was born."

Though the bruises had long ago healed, the memory of that last bout of physical and verbal abuse was still painful. If Thorne could protect Jacob from ever feeling unaccepted or unloved, for whatever reason, he would.

When Thorne had first learned the truth about his own origins, he had blamed his mother for his troubles. Since Pearl had known she was carrying her late husband's child, why had she kept that news from Louis until after they were married? It was little wonder Louis had been hurt and angry as a result. That much was understandable. The only thing Thorne could not forgive was the way the man had treated him as he was growing up in the Ashton mansion. He had no doubt, if it hadn't been for Pearl's intervention, Louis would have tossed him into the streets at the first opportunity and never thought of him again.

In retrospect, incurring Louis's hatred was actually better than enduring his so-called love, Thorne concluded soberly. The old man's interference had probably caused Aaron's death. Even if his brother was still alive, Louis had gotten what he'd wanted. Aaron's little family had been split asunder.

Thorne clenched his fists. If he ever laid eyes on his stepfather again, he was going to have to struggle to control his temper. He knew what the Good Book said; "Vengeance is Mine, I will repay, saith the Lord," but he wasn't the kind of man to stand back and expect a bolt of lightning to come from heaven and handily eliminate his enemies for him.

If such a strike was to end Louis's miserable life, perhaps it was meant to come from the hand of the man he had so often cursed and screamed at in hatred.

Thorne gritted his teeth. Could he kill in cold blood? He strongly doubted it.

Then again, he added with silent determination, if brutality was necessary to protect the lives of Jacob and Naomi—or Charity—he would not hesitate to act in their behalf. Of that he was positive.

He gazed at Jacob through eyes of love. That boy could have been his son. If Naomi had not chosen to wed his brother, her firstborn *would* have been his child.

Struck by the significance of that thought, he stared. His heart leaped. Why had he not seen it before? The darker hair, the deep brown eyes, the stockier body...the child looked a lot more like him than he did Aaron. Had it happened to his family again? Had the wrong man been called "Father"?

He set his jaw, his anger building. If Naomi were in her normal state of mind, she would know. Even if she lied, he felt he'd be able to discern the truth from her words and expression. But now that she was as incapacitated as a babe herself, he might never find out.

Did he really want to know? *Oh, yes.* If he could prove to all concerned that Jacob was not Aaron's son, perhaps he could then convince Louis to leave the boy alone and let him and his mother escape.

Was such a thing possible? Thorne's remembered guilt was intense. He had not meant to sin. Even though he had not seen it as such at the time, he'd understood that what had happened was morally wrong. That was why he had begged Naomi to break off with Aaron and marry him, instead.

She had stolen into his room late at night, after he and Aaron had been drinking heavily to celebrate Aaron's recent betrothal, and had slipped under the covers beside him before he had realized she was even there.

In the ensuing frenzy, Thorne had lost his self-control. He had rued the mistake almost immediately.

"We—we can make it right," Thorne had told her as she had started to leave his bed. "Marry me, Naomi. I can make you happy."

"On a smelly old boat? At sea? Not in a million years." He remembered the scorn in her expression, in her tone. She'd swept her slim, silk-clad arm in an arc that encompassed the lavishly appointed bedroom suite. "I want all this, Thorne. A mansion, money, the prestige of becoming an Ashton of the New York Ashtons."

"Then why did you…?"

"Because you're a beautiful man and I fancied you," she'd said with a half smile. "You're going away tomorrow and I wanted to say a personal goodbye, one I'd never forget."

Thorne had arisen, gathered his things and left the house hours before the rest of the family had awakened. Aaron, however, had followed him to the dock and had insisted on an explanation of why Naomi was sobbing inconsolably and why he was leaving New York so abruptly.

Although Thorne had not gone into detail about their assignation, he had confessed to asking Naomi for her hand in marriage. When Aaron had struck him in response, he had simply stood stoically and accepted the punishment, knowing he deserved much worse.

Later, when he had nearly drowned at sea and had turned to God for salvation, he had repented and had believed his sin was forgiven.

He still believed that. Now, however, it looked as if the consequences of that sin had come back to change his life even more than he'd dreamed. The question was, what was he going to do about it?

Leaning his elbows on the railing of the upper deck, he clasped his hands and stared into the distance at the lighthouse that marked the deep water entrance to the bay. His thoughts spun and wandered like an oarless rowboat caught in a cyclone.

If what he now imagined was true, he was partly responsible. Not only had his indiscretion possibly hindered his brother's marital bliss, it might have created the very reason for Louis's vendetta. Even if the old man did not suspect what Jacob's origins might be, the boy's looks may have reminded him too much of Thorne as a child and therefore predisposed him to feel hatred.

"So, what do I do now, Father," he prayed in a whisper. "What do I do?"

The answer came immediately, not as a spoken word but as a firm assurance. His course was set. He would follow the plan that most benefited his brother's family. Then, if Aaron returned, he'd be able to tell him he had acted honorably. This time.

Chapter Eight

Charity was enough aware of Thorne's moods to realize that he was tormented by something. What could be bothering him, however, was a puzzlement. If anyone in their party had reason to act sad or upset about leaving San Francisco, it should be *her*.

Bidding her father and his intended bride farewell at the hotel had been a heartrending experience. Soft-hearted Annabelle had gotten teary-eyed and even Emory had sniffled when Charity had hugged the two of them goodbye. Their wedding was only a few weeks off but she'd had to depart with Thorne's party so she had promised to celebrate with them when she returned. If she returned.

That recent memory caused her to recall equally reluctant goodbyes when she and her sister had packed all their worldly goods and had left Ohio by wagon train. In the ensuing four years, Charity felt as if she had lived a whole lifetime and was now wise far beyond her true age. Maybe she was. She'd certainly lived through more than enough danger and trauma to last her the remainder of her time on earth.

And *now?* she asked herself. It was foolish to worry about the future when she had no control over it, but her active imagination kept suggesting scenarios right out of her worst nightmares. What if they became separated? What if Naomi wandered off and got lost? What if the man who had attempted to steal Jacob tried again—and succeeded?

Charity tightened her hold on the child until he began to squirm.

She smiled at him. "I'm sorry, sweetheart. I didn't mean to squeeze you too hard. I was just giving you a special hug."

"Okay." Putting his arms back around her neck, he ducked inside the brim of her bonnet and planted a wet kiss on her cheek.

Laughing lightly, she stood at the outside railing on the upper deck and pointed. "Look over there? See the new lighthouse on Alcatraz Island? The light in it had to come all the way across the ocean from France. Maybe one of Uncle Thorne's ships brought it."

"He has sails on his ship," the boy said, looking up at the fluted smokestacks of the steamer. "It's big."

"I know. Did you have fun riding on it?"

"Uh-huh. I even got to turn the wheel."

"Good for you. Was it hard to do?"

The dark curls bounced as he shook his head vigorously. "Nope. Uncle Thorne helped."

"I imagine he did." Grinning, Charity was once again amazed at how quickly the child's zest for life was able to lift her sagging spirits. Seeing the world through his eyes gave everything a lovely quality of newness and a sense of discovery that was missing in the jaded views of most adults, including her.

Watching others waving farewell to loved ones on the docks, she wished her father had been free to come down to the shore to see them off. Unfortunately, Emory and Mrs. Montgomery would be up to their elbows in the hotel kitchen by now, preparing to feed the guests. That kind of endless toil was one part of Charity's daily life in San Francisco that she was positive she would not miss.

Beneath her feet the painted wooden deck trembled from the vibrations of the engine. Pale smoke billowed from the *Grand Republic*'s twin stacks. A shrill whistle near the pilothouse suddenly came alive and blew two long blasts, making her jump.

Seeing the boy's equally wide-eyed response, she was quick to speak. "My, my, that was loud, wasn't it? I think that means we're about to cast off. Shall we go over to the other side and watch the paddle wheel turn?"

"Yeah!"

Charity saw Thorne and Naomi standing together at the far railing as she approached. It was clear from Thorne's posture that he was being protective of the other woman. Charity knew that was as it should be, yet she experienced an unexpected twinge of jealousy.

Instead of surprising them, she announced her arrival with a pleasant, "Hello again. Can we see the paddle wheel from over here? I promised to show it to Jacob."

Thorne stepped aside to make room for her and the boy next to an ornately carved, white-painted post supporting the roof above that portion of the passenger deck. "Take my place," he said. "I've seen it all before."

To Charity's astonishment he stepped close behind her as soon as she had joined Naomi. His presence was so strong, so dizzying, she wondered briefly if she should pass him the child for safety's sake.

Instead, she sat the little boy on the railing with his back to her and held on to him tightly so he wouldn't accidentally slip off.

The *Grand Republic* hissed and moaned and creaked while it slowly backed away from its moorings. Brown pelicans, startled by the noise, took flight from the ends of the piers. Flocks of soaring, diving gulls followed the boat's turbulent wake, squawking and vying for the best positions close to the water.

The paddle wheel soon reversed directions, then picked up speed as the packet boat headed out to sea. It began to lightly splash those passengers brave enough to remain too close. Jacob giggled and swatted at the salty drops.

"We'd better move back," Thorne said. With his arm around Naomi's shoulders, he guided her away through the dispersing crowd.

Charity scooped up the child and followed. She couldn't help noticing that Thorne seemed uneasy, as well as morose.

As soon as he had settled Naomi on a white-painted bench beside the pilothouse, Charity touched his sleeve and drew him aside. "What's wrong?"

"Nothing."

"Don't lie to me, mister. I told you I can tell when a person isn't being truthful. You've been acting strangely ever since we boarded."

He nodded as he scanned the crowd milling around on the passenger deck. "All right. One of our friends from the hotel is also aboard."

She gasped. "Not the man you were chasing!"

"No. Not him. The one who was listening to us talk in the kitchen yesterday."

"He did say he was looking for a boat headed north, too."

"Yes, but…"

"I'd meant to ask what you'd found out this morning and didn't have a good opportunity. Had that man you chased across the roof shown up at the hotel again?"

"No. Nobody has seen hide nor hair of him since yesterday. When the clerk went up to check his room, I went with him. The room was empty except for the usual furnishings. Everything personal was gone."

Her brow knit. "How? If he never came back after he tried to steal Jacob, how could he have gotten upstairs to pick up his belongings?"

"I haven't an earthly idea." Thorne removed his hat and raked his fingers through his thick hair. "Did you notice if he seemed overly friendly with any of the other guests?"

"Such as the one who's on board, you mean?"

"Particularly him."

"I'm afraid not. They may have spoken in passing from time to time but many of our lodgers did that. I never saw those two in the same place except at meals."

"Okay. We'll give him the benefit of the doubt, for the present," Thorne said. "I've had our bags taken to the stateroom I reserved. All except mine, that is. I'll be sleeping in a chair in the saloon with some of the other men."

"You don't have a berth?"

"No. I could only find one available room on a boat that was sailing immediately. Since the episode with Jacob, I thought it was more important to leave quickly than to wait for better accommodations."

"That makes sense." Charity sighed. "All right. I'll need to know where the facility is for our little man pretty soon."

"There'll be a commode in your suite. Use that. I don't want any of you wandering around outside unless it's absolutely necessary." He paused and lowered his voice. "Don't even trust your steward."

She lowered her voice. "Do you still think we're in danger?"

"I don't know. I'd rather assume so and find out I

was being overly cautious than be lax and suffer the consequences, wouldn't you?"

"Yes, of course. It's just that I have never seen the coast and I've heard it's beautiful. I thought it might be enjoyable to watch it pass. If you think it's unwise to do so, I won't venture out."

"I can call for you from time to time," Thorne suggested. "If you don't mind *walking out* with me."

Charity blushed at the intimate connotation of his offer. "I wasn't hinting that I wanted to be treated as if you and I were *courting,* I assure you."

"I know you weren't." He smiled wryly. "If I had thought so, I wouldn't have offered to escort you."

Thorne had guided Charity, Naomi and Jacob to their cabin, made sure the women would lock the door, then had proceeded to the saloon to reconnoiter.

Leaving the damp, still-foggy atmosphere on deck, he entered the interior seating and dining area. Smoke from a multitude of tobacco users was drifting in visible layers that rippled and eddied every time a door was opened and closed.

The saloon was clearly designed more for the usual pleasure of gentlemen than of ladies. Yes, there were side chairs upholstered in red velvet and matching swags with gold braid and tassels decorating the windows, yet the room was definitely a masculine bastion, as witnessed by its almost exclusively male occupants. Most of the men were bellied up to the bar or seated around the small, rimmed

tables and bending an elbow in a show of camaraderie.

Thorne had not taken another drink of whiskey or
any other spirits since the fateful night he and Aaron
had gotten drunk together and Naomi had come between them. The only time being a teetotaler bothered him was in instances like this, where he thought
it best to try to blend in.

He approached the bar and leaned against it side-
ways, not ordering until he was pressed to do so. "A
shot of whatever you're serving," he said, knowing
he wasn't going to actually drink it.

"Yes, sir. Coming up."

Thorne paid the bartender, then nonchalantly fin-
gered his glass while he continued to size up his
fellow travelers. Most were citified, as was to be expected on this first-class level of the steamer. Those
who had to work for their passage or who had been
unable to pay much fare were delegated to the lower
decks, in second and third class, with the cargo and
livestock.

There were friendly card games already underway
at several of the round tables where meals would
later be served to those who could afford them. Judging by the appearances of the players, none was pro-
fessional, although a few seemed to take the games
of chance rather seriously.

"Speaking of serious." Thorne muttered to himself. Looking across the room he easily spotted Cyrus
Satterfield conversing with another individual. The

second man was a shade taller than Satterfield and appeared to be thinner.

Thorne stiffened. Could that be the same man he'd chased over the rooftop? Since both travelers were wearing overcoats it was impossible to tell if the second was as lanky as the scoundrel who had recently tried to abduct Jacob.

Leaving his drink untouched, Thorne strode across the room toward the other men. Now that the *Grand Republic* was underway, there was no avenue of escape, short of jumping overboard and swimming to shore. If this fellow was the one he sought, the one who had bothered his helpless nephew, Thorne was more than prepared to help him leap over the side.

Without introduction or even a polite hello, he grabbed the thinner man by the shoulder and spun him around, much to the astonishment of those passengers standing close by.

Thorne immediately knew he'd made a mistake. This fellow was tall and wiry, all right, but he had a thick, well-waxed mustache that must have taken a year or more to grow and shape so elegantly.

"I'm sorry," Thorne said quickly. "I thought you were someone else."

Giving him the once-over and frowning, the man he had accosted simply walked away. That left Thorne facing only Cyrus Satterfield.

"Do you always come on so strong?" Satterfield asked.

"If I think I need to."

"Well," he said, chuckling wryly, "in that case, remind me to stay out of your way."

"Leave my sister-in-law alone and we'll have no more trouble," Thorne told him.

"My error." The thickset man gave a slight bow and arched an eyebrow. "I had understood that the lady was a widow or I never would have offered her my arm."

"*If* my brother is dead, and I'm not saying that he is, his widow is my concern, not yours."

"Not a very friendly attitude," Satterfield said, tipping his head back to blow smoke into the already-thick atmosphere. "But have it your way. The widow is all yours."

The last was spoken with a sneer that was almost insulting enough to prompt Thorne to take a swing at the pompous fool. He refrained. No sense getting into a melee and drawing attention to himself or his party. If Satterfield was a man of his word and did keep his distance, no further action would be necessary.

If he broke his promise to leave Naomi alone, however, Thorne was more than ready to impress him with his folly, to whatever degree the situation demanded.

Charity was still tense and jumpy and the closeness of the tiny cabin did nothing to soothe her nerves. Neither did the restless little boy. The projected journey of six or seven days and nights promised to be most trying. Although she was able to catch glimpses of the passing terrain as the sun rose and eventually burned off the coastal fog, she couldn't see nearly enough to satisfy her curiosity. Or Jacob's.

Finally she decided to don her shawl, open the cabin door and stand there with him in her arms so they could both safely observe the changing landscape.

Beams of the rising sun bathed the coastal hills in golden-green light. Mighty live oaks stood in groves like sentinels over the vast ocean beyond their shores.

There was raw beauty in the ruggedness of the coast with very little evidence that man had altered God's handiwork. Here and there, Charity caught a glimpse of what could have been signs of settlers or Indians but by and large the landscape was unsullied.

She was still marveling at the passing scenery when Thorne appeared on deck and approached her.

"I thought you promised to stay in your cabin," he said gruffly.

"I'm sort of in it," Charity countered with a sheepish grin. "At least my heels are inside."

"I meant with the door locked, and you know it."

"Yes, I know. It's just so stuffy in there and so beautiful out here." Shifting Jacob to her other hip she pointed. "Look at those rocks. And that cliff! It's so steep. Every couple of miles the terrain seems to change to something altogether new."

"Those are the famous redwoods of California you see up there," Thorne said, swinging his arm and pointing. "They don't grow anywhere else in the world, that I know of."

"I've seen the wood, of course, but I've never had

the pleasure of seeing a live tree still standing. I've heard they're very impressive."

"They are. Maybe someday you'll have the chance to view them more closely."

"Maybe." She grew subdued. "Who knows what the future holds?"

"God does," Thorne said with conviction.

"You really believe that?"

"Yes, I do." He held out his arms to relieve her of Jacob. "You look tired. Let me hold him for a while."

"Thank you."

Thinking of all the trauma and tribulations she'd faced while crossing the plains, Charity was moved to speak her mind. "Why do you feel that God even cares?" she asked. "I mean, with all the evil in the world, how can you possibly say that?"

"I don't know. I'm no theologian. I can't explain it to myself so I'm pretty sure I can't make it clear to you, either. All I do know is that when I was shipwrecked and positive I was about to draw my last breath, I called out to God in desperation and He gave me peace for whatever happened. I wasn't even sure I was going to be rescued. I simply knew I was safely in the Lord's hands, no matter what."

"Is that why you're still holding out hope that your brother survived? Because *you* did?"

"Partly, I suppose." He smiled wistfully. "It is my fondest wish that Aaron and his family will find happiness again."

Empathetic, Charity lightly touched his sleeve on

the arm that was supporting the child. "The Good Book does mention children as being special. If you're right about God looking after all of us, I imagine He's even more tenderhearted toward these innocent little ones."

"As are you," Thorne told her. "I don't know what we'd do, how we'd manage without you, Miss Beal."

"It is fortunate that you chose to stop at the Montgomery House."

"Fortunate?" Raising one eyebrow, he began to smile. "I would much rather consider it providential, although that may be a gross understatement. Now that I've given the matter more thought, I would say that you're definitely part of the Lord's plan for me."

His words took Charity's breath away for an instant, until he added, "And my family."

Chapter Nine

Jacob had fallen asleep in his uncle's arms so Thorne had carried him inside and laid him tenderly on an empty berth, then had bid the women a polite good-afternoon.

Charity hadn't expected to see hide nor hair of him again until morning so she was surprised when someone rapped loudly and insistently on her cabin door a few hours later. She laid aside her daily journal and pencil and went to answer the knock.

Cautious and more than a little tremulous, she grasped the knob, leaned against the thin wooden door and called, "Who is it?"

"Me."

Her relief at hearing the familiar rumble of Thorne's voice was so great it left her a bit giddy. "I beg your pardon, sir. I don't know anyone by that name."

Giggling, she listened to his masculine mutterings for a few seconds before she unlocked the door and peeked out. "Oh, it's you. Why didn't you say so?"

"I thought I did."

She swung the door wide and studied his face. "So, you did. What's the matter? You look concerned."

"Not overly so. We're putting in at a cove for the night and I thought I should explain what was going on. The weather promises to worsen and the coast is getting pretty rugged up this way. Our captain doesn't want to chance running aground on the rocks or getting the wheel or rudder fouled on the kelp that breaks loose during rough weather. I happen to agree with his assessment."

"Will we be safe?" Charity asked.

"Safer than we'd be on the open sea in this small craft." He smiled at her. "How are you all doing?"

She huffed. "Well, since you've asked, Naomi insists she's seasick and has taken to her bed. Jacob only dozed for a few minutes after you left us and refuses to nap anymore, so he's grumpier than a hibernating bear in January. And I have a pounding headache, all of which I have duly recorded in my daily journal. Therefore, I'd have to say we're coping, as usual."

He wouldn't have laughed in response if Charity hadn't been grinning wryly. "Glad to hear everything is normal."

"I knew you would be. Any more sign of the man you were worried about?"

"No. He hasn't shown up in the saloon since I confronted him and I haven't been able to locate him anywhere else on the boat."

"Then that's good, right?"

"In a manner of speaking. I'd almost rather have him underfoot than have to wonder what else he may be up to."

"You are a hard man to please."

Thorne's smile grew. "You're just now figuring that out? Tsk-tsk. I thought you were smarter than that."

"Smart enough to try to stay on your good side," she quipped. "Listen, is there any chance we could get a light meal? It doesn't have to be fancy. Jacob has eaten all the food I brought along and I'm starving."

"Sorry. I should have explained. I've already arranged with the galley for your meals to be served in your suite. Would you like me to dine with you or would you prefer your privacy?"

Charity chuckled. "Privacy? In here? It feels more like solitary confinement. I—we—would love to have you eat with us."

"In that case, I'll be back in a jiffy." He paused and stared pointedly at her. "Lock the door again and keep it locked until I get back."

"You worry too much."

Thorne's brow furrowed and his eyes narrowed. "It's not unreasonable to worry if someone is really after you," he said flatly. "Lock that door. Now."

As he turned to go he heard the click of the lock. She might think he was overreacting but he knew better. Any of Louis Ashton's prior reprehensible deeds would have been enough to convince Thorne that nothing short of death would stop the old man from carrying out his plans to eliminate Aaron's family.

The way Thorne saw it, he was the only deterrent standing between that family and an untimely death. He, and Charity Beal.

He knew he couldn't have asked for a more dedicated, loyal ally.

Charity was perplexed. She stood in the center of the cabin and tried to figure out where they should spread their repast. The closer the boat drew to the shore the choppier the water became and although she and Jacob seemed fine, poor Naomi lay in her narrow berth, moaning.

Finally, Charity decided it would be wiser to relocate the small wooden writing desk and use it for a table than to leave it where it was in the cramped cabin. If she dragged it out onto the deck, she reasoned, they could breathe fresh air as they supped and no one would have to listen to Naomi's laments.

She had nearly finished relocating the makeshift dining table and two armless side chairs when Thorne reappeared. She could tell by his expression of disgust that he wasn't pleased by her choice of arrangements.

"Don't look at me like that." Charity faced him with her hands fisted on her hips. "I imagine it won't bother an old salt like you but there is a very ill woman in my cabin and I don't relish the notion of having to try to eat while in the same room with her. It wouldn't be good for Jacob, either."

Thorne nodded and acquiesced. "You're right. Naomi is definitely not a sailor. She hardly ate a bite during our entire voyage around the horn. Aaron plied her with sugar cubes dosed in peppermint oil but she remained ill in spite of it."

"Poor thing. No wonder she seems so frail," Charity said. "I'll see if I can coax her into eating a sop of bread or chewing on some gingerroot, later. We should be better off once we've stopped, right?"

"As a matter of fact, we're already at anchor."

"But how can we be? I still hear the engine."

"The captain is keeping the boilers fired up to counter the tide when it turns. That way, we can also be underway as soon as he deems it safe. It's a wise decision."

"I see. There's certainly a lot to know about running a boat, isn't there?"

"Or a sailing ship," Thorne said. He carefully placed a basket of food on the deck. "You might want to bring a blanket outside and we'll make this a picnic. Keeping everything on the top of that little desk in this weather will be nigh impossible. Dishes were sliding off the tables in the saloon just now, even though those are made with rimmed edges."

"Well, why didn't you say so before? It took me ages to drag that cumbersome thing outside."

"Then stay put and watch the boy. I'll put it back for you."

"Nonsense. I can handle it."

"I know you can, but…" He bent over and reached for the edges of the desk at the same time Charity did.

Their heads bumped and their hands overlapped, his atop hers. His touch was firm and reassuring.

Instead of giving ground or jumping away, she froze and tilted her head to look at him. At the same instant Thorne's gaze met hers. His face was mere inches from hers and she could feel his warm breath on her cheeks, on her lips.

Looking into his dark brown eyes, she was struck by their unexpected intensity, their emotional impact on her very being. Charity imagined it would be easy to drown in the all-encompassing depths of his gaze.

Finally, after what had seemed like aeons, she came to her senses, slipped her hands free, straightened and stepped back. Thorne made no comment.

Instead of following him into the cabin while he replaced the desk and chairs, Charity called, "There's an extra blanket folded at the foot of my berth. Bring that one for us to sit on? Please?"

Remaining silent, he did as she asked, handed her the blanket, then stood aside while she spread it on the deck.

Except for cautious peeks at him through lowered lashes, Charity kept her gaze averted. She wondered if Thorne's emotions had been as affected by their accidental proximity as hers were. She doubted it. After all, he was a man of the world, a successful ship owner and veteran traveler. He had seen faraway places and had certainly met many women much prettier, more educated and more interesting than a simple farm girl from Ohio.

No, her heart corrected, *not a girl, a woman.* A woman who was once married, sullied by cruelty, and therefore ruined for any good, normal man who might someday come along and wish to become her husband.

Thorne knew all about that part of her history, she reminded herself. Little wonder he had said he wasn't going to take her walking the way a suitor might and was now acting reluctant to even look at her again, let alone purposely take her hand, which was just as well. Thanks to the painful memories of Ramsey Tucker's abuse, she normally recoiled from any grown man's touch, except perhaps that of her own father.

Now, however, Charity was puzzled. Something very troubling had just occurred and she wasn't prepared to deal with it. Although she realized that Thorne had merely covered her hands with his by accident rather than purposefully, she had not been repulsed by the contact. Not in the slightest.

Admitting that startling fact, even to herself, was almost as frightening as their continued flight from would-be assassins.

The simple meal of cold meat, bread, cheese and canned peaches had been quickly completed. Since the weather was worsening and rain had begun to dot the deck beyond the sheltering overhang, Thorne had bid them good-night, picked up the basket and politely taken his leave.

Bone weary, Charity had seen to Jacob's personal needs, then had done as much as she could for Naomi, including making her a weak ginger tea out of tepid water to settle her stomach. Adding a drop of laudanum to the tea had helped Naomi relax and sleep.

Although no one had actually dressed for bed due to the dangers inherent in the inclement weather, Charity had loosened her clothing and slipped off her shoes and stockings before lying down.

She forced herself to close her eyes as she listened to the creaking of the wooden craft and the drum of activity belowdecks. Every so often there was also a long, drawn-out hiss which she attributed to the venting of excess steam.

Recalling Jacob's bedtime antics, Charity smiled to herself. Due to the narrowness of the berths she had said, "I'll make you your very own bed and we'll slide it under mine. That way you'll still be close by and your mother and I won't step on you if we have to get up during the night. How does that sound?"

When he'd answered, "No," and started to whine she'd realized she should not have posed the idea as a question.

"I want to sleep with you, in a real bed," he had insisted, sniffling and rubbing his eyes with his fists.

"Okay, if that's what you want." Charity chose her words more carefully this time. "But these berths are awfully narrow for two. I thought you'd like making your very own cabin. We could have fun pretending it's a fort or a cave—and you could even be a bear."

"Really?" Pout forgotten, his dark eyes had sparkled. "A bear? A big bear?"

"Yes. Of course, if you don't want to…"

"I do, I do." He'd dropped to his hands and knees to peer into the narrow space. "Make me a cave."

As soon as she had prepared his pallet, he had gladly shinnied onto it and had quickly discovered an added bonus to his make-believe den. Roaring as if he were a real bear, he'd begun kicking at the bottom side of her thin mattress and giggling when she'd pretended to be scared.

They had laughed and teased for a few minutes until she had dimmed the lamp and he had dozed off. So had Naomi. Charity was heartened to hear the other woman's soft sighs in the nearly dark cabin. At least the poor dear was no longer moaning and tossing about. That was certainly something to be thankful for.

With both her charges finally in repose, Charity was free to begin to unwind. She began by saying her prayers, then let her mind drift beyond the confines of the cabin and imagined herself standing on the shore amid the towering trees Thorne had pointed out.

Unfortunately, once she fell asleep and began to dream, her lovely visions became tortured and filled with her late husband's threats and cruelty. Her heart pounded. Beads of perspiration dotted her forehead and neck. She saw herself running blindly in the midst of a whirling, punishing tornado like the one that had leveled their Ohio farm and killed her mother.

In the nightmare, Charity was fleeing from an ugliness too foul, too indescribable to even have a face, yet she knew who it was. Who it had to be. Though Ramsey Tucker was dead, the memory of him continued to haunt her.

She called out to God in her terror. Suddenly her eyes popped open. She blinked rapidly. Torrential rain was beating against a small window with such alarming ferocity it seemed sure to break through the fragile glass at any moment.

For a few seconds Charity didn't remember where she was or with whom. It was the rocking and pitching of the room that reminded her. She threw aside her blanket and swung her feet to the floor while she fought to calm down and regain her sensibilities.

"I'm on a steamboat," she whispered, rubbing her eyes. "I'm safe. We're safe. This cabin is secure and everyone is fine."

She strained to listen, to reassure herself. All she could hear was the rapid beating of her own pulse, the creaking of the wooden hull, and the incessant hammering of the deluge against the walls and tin roof.

Her lamp had apparently gone out while she slept. She reached for the place she was certain she had left it and touched thin air, instead.

Lightning flashed. Thunder shook the cabin.

Charity blinked and tried to focus, wishing the burst of light had lasted longer so she could get her bearings.

Whatever had she done with that lamp? It couldn't have fallen to the floor or she'd smell spilled coal oil.

Standing, she extended her arms and groped across the short distance to Naomi's berth. Her knees bumped against the railing along the side.

She bent cautiously, wary of losing her balance and falling against the other women. Her hands touched the blankets. They were warm. Rumpled.

Charity patted the surface of the berth, then slapped it more vigorously.

Her breath caught as she realized there was no doubt. The bed was empty. Naomi was gone!

Thorne was dozing with his feet propped on one of the red velvet chairs, his torso half reclining in another, when he felt icy drops of water hitting his face. Someone was shaking his shoulders. Someone very wet.

He opened his eyes, ready to snap at whoever had disturbed him. It was Charity. Her hair was plastered to her cheeks and neck and her clothing was soaked. One look at her wild-eyed expression brought him to immediate alertness.

"What is it? What's happened?"

"Naomi's gone!"

"When? How?"

"I don't know." She shivered and wrapped her arms around herself to fend off the chill. "I didn't hear a thing. I just woke up and she was gone."

"What about the boy?" When she didn't immediately respond, Thorne was sorely tempted to give her a shake.

"He's—he's fine. I think," she finally said.

"You locked the door when you left him, right? *Right?*"

Her expression of utter terror and confusion was all the answer Thorne needed. He was out the saloon door and running along the deck before he'd made a conscious decision to do so. One quick glance over his shoulder told him that Charity was following.

He jerked open the cabin door and fumbled to strike a match. His heart fell. All the berths were empty.

Whirling, he pulled Charity inside and demanded, "What happened? Tell me exactly what you remember?"

"Nothing."

Thorne could tell she was fighting tears but he didn't have time to coddle her. "There must be something. Think. What woke you?"

"A—a nightmare. I dreamed I was running away and it was raining. There was terrible wind, like a tornado."

"Your mind may have been prompted to think that when the door was opened and you felt the storm blowing in on you from outside. Did you rise immediately?"

"Yes. I couldn't find the lamp. I thought I knew where I had left it but it wasn't there, so I felt my way across the room to check on Naomi. She was gone."

Thorne could hear the catch in Charity's voice,

sense the pathos she was feeling. "All right," he said. "You can't go running around out on deck like that or you'll have the ague by morning. Put on your heavy coat to keep warm and we'll rouse the crew to help us look. Naomi must have taken Jacob with her. Chances are we'll find them together."

"No. Wait," Charity shouted. She fell to her knees and reached beneath her berth. "He's here! Praise, God, Jacob's still here."

Thorne joined her as she eased the sleepy child out from his hiding place and enfolded him in her embrace. More lightning revealed that tears were sliding down her cheeks. He could understand her emotional response. His was similar.

He swallowed hard past the lump in his throat before he asked, "What was he doing under there?"

"Pretending to be a—a bear," she stuttered. "I didn't want him to get stepped on if I had to get up in the night to see to Naomi so I talked him into sleeping out of the way. I—I was just trying to be practical. I never dreamed it would keep him safe the way it did."

The little boy had wrapped his arms around Charity's damp neck, as if clinging to a life preserver. Thorne wanted to hold him, too, but decided to leave him right were he was, safe and secure in the tender-hearted woman's embrace.

Instead, he leaned closer and asked, "Are you all right, Jacob?"

"Uh-huh." The child seemed to be looking over

Charity's shoulder and searching the darkness. "Is he gone?"

"Is *who* gone?" Thorne asked.

"The man. The bad man. I saw him but I was scared to holler." He began to sniffle. "I'm sorry, Uncle Thorne."

"There's nothing to be sorry about," he answered, taking care to temper his tone so the child wouldn't become more frightened. "Did you see what happened? Did he take your mama away?"

The tousled head nodded vigorously.

"What did he look like?"

"I don't know. He had on a real shiny coat."

"Black, like the captain and crew wear?"

"I think so." Jacob yawned. "Will you go get Mama, Uncle Thorne? She shouldn't be out in the rain."

"No, she certainly shouldn't." He looked to Charity. "You stay here with him and lock the door after me."

"What good will that do? I had it locked and someone got in anyway."

"Humor me." Reaching into his pocket, he withdrew a tiny pistol barely as big as his palm. "Here. It only has two shots, one in each barrel, but it's better than nothing."

Cautious, he held it out and waited until she accepted it. "Don't be afraid, just be careful," Thorne said. "It won't fire unless you cock it first, so it's safe enough. Make sure you don't point it at anything or anybody unless you intend to shoot."

"I don't think I could purposely hurt anyone."

"Could you if they were threatening the boy?" Watching her expression change to one of resolution and seeing her nod, he was satisfied she'd be capable of defending his nephew if need be.

"That's what I thought," Thorne said. "All right. I'll go do what I can to find Naomi."

Charity grabbed his sleeve as he turned to leave. "How can I help?"

"Pray," Thorne said without hesitation. "Pray harder than you ever have before. I'm going to need divine intervention. And so is Naomi."

Chapter Ten

Wind pushed wave after wave of rain in blinding sheets, driving it nearly parallel to the decks of the pitching steamer.

The man struggling across the slippery starboard deck with an unwilling, groggy woman in tow was having trouble keeping his feet. It galled him that he hadn't been able to locate the child, too, and make short work of them both. Oh, well. As soon as he managed to drag his burden farther aft and hurl her over that railing, he'd be half done. That was enough to crow about.

He had taken the only lamp from the Ashton woman's cabin, then had decided it was too much bother and had tried to toss it into the ocean. When he'd heard its glass breaking against a lower deck he'd realized he'd have to drag his victim to the rear of the craft to make sure she dropped directly into the icy water. After all, in a storm like this, accidents were bound to happen.

A shout echoed above the sound of thunder and the crashing of waves. Another followed. He could hear the clomp of several pairs of boots running along the deck. Although the rain masked much of the sound, he suspected his deed had been discovered and he was being pursued.

Pausing, he hit the woman in the jaw to stun her more, then released his hold and let her fall to the deck. If he was lucky, maybe she'd slip when she tried to get up and the rolling of the waves would cause her to plummet overboard without his help. If not, he'd simply try again. It wasn't as if Louis Ashton would ever know he'd failed. Nor would he reveal his inability to locate the boy in the darkened cabin.

Lightning flashed. He saw shadowy forms racing toward him. Ducking around the port side below the pilothouse, he shed his long, black slicker just as he darted through a narrow doorway leading to a back passage into the saloon.

"The fools have underestimated me," he muttered, satisfied that his ruse had worked and pleased that he'd had the foresight to scout out an alternate way to reach the cabin he had chosen to occupy.

He laughed softly at his wit as he reminded himself that the cabin's previous owner had been far too dead to object when he had tossed his carcass over the side earlier.

Straightening his clothing, Cyrus Satterfield

brushed off his coat sleeves, then smoothed what was left of his reddish hair over his partially balding head. There were times, like now, when he was glad he didn't have a thick head of hair to deal with or try to keep dry. As it was, any slickness of his pate would be taken for pomade, not water, and nobody would be the wiser.

He sidled into the ship's saloon, intending to merely pass through. Unfortunately, all the ruckus on deck had awakened others. Rather than appear furtive, he decided to simply join the group as if equally concerned.

Nodding politely, he approached a crewman at the bar. "What's going on? I thought I heard shouts. We aren't sinking, are we?"

"Naw," the man drawled. "Some fool woman got herself lost and the cap'n was hollerin' for volunteers." He guffawed. "You won't see me riskin' my neck out on deck in this storm if I don't have to. No sirree."

"I see. Has there been any word of her yet?"

"Not directly. I suppose they found her 'cause the yellin's stopped. Stupid woman. Never should allow the likes of them on board if you ask me. I'll be plumb glad when she gets off at Astoria."

Satterfield perked up. "Astoria? I thought they…"

"Beg pardon?"

"Nothing. Are you sure she's getting off?" He forced a nonchalant air and a smile. "I mean, the sooner the better if she's such a poor sailor, right?"

"Yeah. Cap'n Nash said the folks in her party was headed up the Columbia a ways, so I suppose they'll go ashore when we dock there. We're bound for Puget, up north."

"I know. I had thought to sail all the way with you. How long does that leg of the journey usually take?"

"A lot longer than it should, once we leave the mouth of the Columbia River. Lots of rocks and little islands out there, not to mention the bar. Real tricky to navigate. But don't you worry. We don't draw much more'n five or six feet of draft fully loaded and our captain's a wonder with the charts. Never seen him make a mistake."

Before Satterfield could comment the door burst open and another crewman entered, bringing news of the rescue.

Pretending to listen and feigning shock at word of the heinous crime, Cyrus smiled to himself. There would be another day soon. Another chance. As long as he never gave up, he *would* be successful.

Thorne had been the first to come upon Naomi. He'd found her lying on the deck and curled into a fetal position.

He'd lifted her gently and supported her by the shoulders. When she had opened her eyes and taken one look at him, she had fainted dead away.

Scooping her up in his arms, he had assured the other searchers that she was in good hands and had headed for her cabin. Not able to knock easily, he gave the door a swift kick and shouted, "Miss Beal. Open the door."

The instant she did, he shouldered through.

Charity gasped. "Is she all right?"

"I think so. She's swooned but she's breathing well."

"Put her on the bed." She turned to reassure the worried little boy. "Mama's fine, honey. She's just a little woozy right now."

Thorne stepped back. If the man who had tried to abduct Naomi had been dressed like one of the packet boat's crew, did that mean a crewman was also on Louis's payroll? The possibility was strong.

"She's coming around," Charity said as she vigorously rubbed Naomi's hands and forearms and patted her cheeks.

"Good. I'm going to go talk to the captain and see if he can shed any light on who might have access to rain gear besides his men. Will you two be all right alone?"

"We aren't alone." Charity smiled at Jacob. "We have each other and now that his mama is back with us, we'll be just fine. As soon as you leave I'll get her wet clothes off her and make sure she's good and warm."

"Lock the door after me," Thorne ordered.

"Don't you ever get tired of telling me that?" she asked, rolling her eyes.

All he said was, "No."

Disgusted with herself for failing to watch Naomi well enough and mad at Thorne for being so brusque about the whole situation, Charity made a droll face at his departing figure.

To her surprise, Jacob mirrored her comical expression. She couldn't help but laugh. "It's okay to do that this time, honey, but I don't think you should make funny faces at Uncle Thorne again."

"Why?"

Charity giggled, carrying on the conversation with him while she also undressed his shivering, uncommunicative mother. "Because it's really not polite. Besides, he might ask you where you learned to do it and you'd have to tell him the truth. I don't want him to be angry with me for teaching you something bad. Understand?"

"Uh-huh. Can I go back under the bed and be a bear again?"

"I think that's a wonderful idea," Charity said with a tender smile. "And if you see that bad man again, I want you to tell me or your uncle right away. All right?"

"I could roar and scare him away," the child said, demonstrating by forming his pudgy fingers into claws and giving his best growl.

"Why don't we just let Uncle Thorne do that for us? He might feel bad if we took his job."

"What job?"

"Why, the one as our brave protector," Charity said, realizing that she meant every word. "Uncle Thorne is doing his best to take good care of all of us."

"Even you?"

"Yes, even me." She tucked the covers around the still-dazed woman and straightened.

"Good. 'Cause I love you, Miss Charity."

She leaned down and placed a kiss on the top of Jacob's head. "I know you do, dear. And I love you, too."

"How 'bout Uncle Thorne?"

"I'm sure he loves you, too, Jacob."

"I mean, you. Does he love you?"

Blushing, Charity searched her heart for the right words before she spoke. "I just work for him, taking care of you and your mama while we travel. That's why he wants to keep me safe, too."

"I think he likes you," Jacob said with a grin, before he whirled and skipped back to his pretend cave. He stuck his head out from under the bed to add, "You're real pretty."

"Thank you, dear."

The child's innocent praise made her doubly aware of the sorry state of her damp hair and clothing. She had no doubt Thorne Blackwell had been unimpressed by her so-called beauty when she'd raced out into the downpour to fetch him. On the contrary, some of the soggy chickens penned on the cargo deck probably looked far more presentable than she did at the moment.

That comparison made her chuckle to herself. There was a time, long ago, when her appearance had been all she'd thought about. Her hair had to be curled and arranged just so, her dresses had to be spotless and crisply ironed, and the lace hems on her petticoats had to be as white as a summer cloud. Until her trip across the plains with her older sister, she had never gone out in the sun without a hat or a bonnet, either, yet by the time she had reached California she was sporting the freckles that still dusted her nose and rosy cheeks.

It no longer mattered to her whether or not her complexion was flawless or her hair a silky gold. As long as she was clean and did the best she could with what she had, she didn't obsess about her looks.

The state of disorder she was currently displaying was another matter, however. She owed it to her employer, and to his family, to make herself as presentable as possible.

She sighed. It was difficult to tell the time without a watch but she felt as if dawn must surely be approaching. Assuming that to be so, she would don dry clothing and do what she could with her own hair before trying to rouse Naomi and helping her do the same.

In the back of Charity's mind was the niggling doubt that she was not polishing her public image totally because of her job. Like it or not, she wanted to look more than respectable.

She wanted to look pretty.

For Thorne Blackwell.

There were plenty of men still milling around in the saloon by the time Thorne joined them. He immediately noted that Cyrus Satterfield was present. So was the boat's captain and some of the crew.

Ignoring the inquiring looks of others, Thorne went straight to the captain. "I'm glad I caught you,

Captain Nash. I was on my way to the pilothouse to ask if any of your men was missing a slicker. I just found this one lying on the deck." He held up the shiny coat and watched water drip off it. "Can you tell whose it is?"

Nash shook his head. "Standard issue, I'm afraid, sir. Why?"

"Because my nephew says the man who took his mother was wearing one like it. I thought he'd still have it on but apparently he shed it outside."

"I'm sure none of my men was responsible. They're all totally trustworthy."

"I'm sure they are. Would you mind asking if any of them are missing this coat?"

"I could ask," the captain said, "but I'm not going to. Your party has been reunited and all is well. I don't want my crew all riled up for nothing."

"For nothing?" Thorne didn't try to hide his displeasure. He shook the coat for emphasis and more drops scattered. "I hardly consider this nothing."

"Nevertheless…" Turning, the captain walked away and left the saloon, ending the discussion.

Thorne held up the coat again and queried the crowd. "Do any of you know anything about this? There'll be a reward for information on who was wearing this slicker tonight."

To Thorne's disgust and dismay, the only man who paid attention to his offer was Cyrus Satterfield.

Edging his way along the bar, Satterfield raised an eyebrow and smiled. "I guess they're not that interested in earning a reward," he said. "I, however, might be. What sum did you have in mind?"

Thorne was hesitant to name a figure so he hedged. "Are you saying you know something about this?"

"No. But I'm willing to ask around and see what I can come up with if you'll make it worth my while."

"Forget it," Thorne told him. "I can do that myself."

"Have it your way. Well, I guess I'll be getting back to my cabin since all the excitement is over."

That simple declaration raised the hackles on the back of Thorne's neck. He scowled. "Hold on. How did you get a cabin? I booked passage before you did and I was only able to reserve one."

"Perhaps I'm luckier than you are," the heavyset man said with a snide expression and a wave. "Good night."

Watching him leave the saloon, Thorne remained puzzled. He supposed he could query the captain about Satterfield's cabin. If he disclosed his own background at sea and encouraged camaraderie, he might get better cooperation. Unfortunately, since he didn't want to reveal his true identity, even to Captain Nash, that wasn't feasible. Nor was it wise.

Given his working knowledge of shipboard politics and loyalties, Thorne knew who else to ask. There wasn't a ship's cook on the high seas who didn't know everything that went on belowdecks. Hopefully, the same would be true on the smaller packet boat.

Thorne toted the slicker with him as he headed for

the galley. As expected, he found members of the crew already hard at work preparing upcoming meals. The overheated room was heavy with the pleasant aroma of cooking and the less appealing odor of the provisions that had been spilled and wasted during the storm and were now being trod underfoot through the wooden grating. If he had been captain of the *Grand Republic* he'd have insisted the galley crew clean the place before doing anything else.

He'd met the chief cook for the first time when he'd picked up the evening meal for Charity and Jacob so he made straight for him.

"Food's not ready yet," the cook said, wiping his brow with his soiled muslin apron. "Be another hour, at least."

"I wasn't looking for something to eat," Thorne said. "You have lists of all the passengers in the cabins and what meals they've requested, don't you?"

"Yeah. You wanna make a change?"

"No, no. I was just wondering if I could take a peek at the list and make sure it's right." He forced a grin. "Wouldn't want the little woman to miss her tea or something and fuss at me for it."

"Long as she don't fuss at me," the cook said with a huff. He pointed. "Book's over there in that drawer. Have a look-see. Just make it snappy and be sure you put it back like it was when you're through."

"Certainly."

Thorne draped the slicker over his shoulders as if it were his and retrieved the ledger. Large lamps

swung from the rafters, just as they had on his ship.
He braced his feet on the still-pitching deck and
oriented himself to the light to read.

He scanned the list twice. Nowhere did it mention
anyone named Cyrus Satterfield occupying a cabin.
Either the man was lying about his accommodations
or he'd been lying about his name. Or both.

Chapter Eleven

The *Grand Republic* had hoisted anchor and headed back out to sea that morning as the weather had cleared and the sun had begun to peek over the hills to the east.

Although the paddle wheeler had continued to skirt the coast as before, she'd occasionally had to pull farther from shore for safety's sake, or so Thorne had explained.

Charity didn't care what the boat did as long as it continued to steam steadily northward. She knew they'd make stops along the way to pick up and deliver more mail and freight but she didn't want to delay any longer than was absolutely necessary.

Now that Naomi had recovered from her seasickness during the storm and was acting healthier, the poor woman had resumed her previous state of befuddlement, much to Charity's dismay.

Jacob had gotten to the point where he seldom tried to converse with his mother, preferring to bring his needs and interests to Charity's attention, instead. She understood why. She just wished he could relate better to his own mama.

Keeping the restless, curious child occupied was far more difficult aboard the steamer than it had been on land. Finally, in desperation, Charity had insisted they take regular turns around the passenger deck as a group, weather permitting.

To her surprise and delight, Thorne had chosen to join them. It was a true relief to have an extra pair of eyes watching the rambunctious little boy. Jacob seldom met a stranger and he got into more than his share of mischief. He also delighted in finding older adults to talk to and had to be reined in quite often. It seemed as if he never tired, never slowed down except to sleep.

The farther north the *Grand Republic* took them, the more rainy and cloudy the weather became. Because Charity was used to the moderate temperatures in San Francisco, this part of the country chilled her to the bone. If she had not had the exuberant child and her other chores to occupy her mind, she feared the dank weather would have seriously dampened her spirits, as well.

Sitting on deck with Naomi and watching Thorne and Jacob play tag like two children, Charity couldn't help smiling. In her mind's eye she could see that Thorne would make a fine father some day. He was firm but patient, never too busy to explain anything the little boy asked about.

When Jacob dashed up to her, grabbed her hand and tried to tug her to the railing, she laughed. "What's so important, dear?"

"The big river! Come look. We're almost there!"

Charity stood, wrapped the too-large overcoat more tightly around her and urged Naomi to come along. "It must be the mouth of the Columbia," she told the other woman. "That means our journey at sea is nearly over. Aren't you excited? Let's go see."

Although Naomi rose, Charity could tell she wasn't totally comprehending. What a pity. All Charity could hope for at this point was that the presence of Naomi's mother and father would help restore her to the whole person she had been before Aaron's abduction.

Charity sighed. Even if Naomi didn't recover, at least dear little Jacob would be with grandparents who would love him. If she had thought otherwise, she would have wept for him constantly.

Taking a place beside Thorne at the starboard railing, Charity smiled. He had scooped up the child and was pointing to a broad expanse of water in the distance.

"Over there," Thorne said. "See how the color is different? That's where the fresh water and saltwater come together."

Charity shaded her eyes against the sun's glare. "It's so wide. I never would have imagined anything so large being a river. It looks more like an extension of the ocean."

"Parts of it are saltwater, depending on the tide,"

he said. "Larger ships have to wait for high tides to sail across the bar or they may go aground on the shifting sand. It can be treacherous."

"Once they get across are they safe?"

"Yes, except for the storms that arise so often up here."

"I can see that sailing is a terribly dangerous occupation," Charity said with concern. "I shall worry about you from now on."

Speaking from the heart without censoring her thoughts, she realized belatedly that he was staring at her. She met his compelling gaze.

"Will you? Truly?" he asked quietly.

"Of course."

"I believe you mean that."

Totally absorbed in the tenderness of his expression, she was unable to make herself look away. She had to pause for several heartbeats to gather her wits before she said, "Of course I do."

"As I will also worry about you. This has been the easy part of our journey," Thorne said soberly. "From now on it may be even more hazardous. I wish…"

Charity could only imagine what he had been going to say. "What?" she asked. "What do you wish?"

Her slim hand was resting on the railing. Thorne shifted Jacob to the opposite side, then placed his hand over Charity's as he said, "I wish I had not urged you to come with us."

Startled, she stared. "Because you think me incompetent?"

"No." His brow furrowed, his dark gaze growing even more enthralling. "Because you have become so important to me, Miss Beal."

Before she could form a coherent reply he'd released her hand and stepped back.

"Forgive me," he said formally. "I had no right to speak to you that way. It was unseemly."

But lovely, she added to herself. *So lovely.* She would not encourage him by expressing that thought, of course. To do so would be unfair. She was never going to allow herself to remarry and accepting anything less was unthinkable.

Still, she told herself, turning away to gaze at the entrance to the mighty Columbia River gorge, if she ever were to consider giving another man a special place in her heart, that man would have to be a lot like Thorne Blackwell.

It had been easy to befriend him, she admitted. And to trust him as an ally. But there was far more to marriage than standing at the railing of a steamboat and having a pleasant conversation. It wasn't the overt parts of a relationship she feared, it was the hidden parts, the intimacies she knew she could never again bear, no matter how tender her husband's touch might be.

The mere thought of being under a man's control gave her the shivers and made her stomach turn. Four years ago, she had sworn she would never again allow herself to become anyone else's possession. Anyone's chattel. There was much in life which confused her but about *that,* she was adamant.

"I'll take Jacob back to your cabin. Will you see to Naomi?" Thorne asked.

Charity nodded. She wouldn't look at him, couldn't look at him, because she was certain her anguish and abhorrence would show and he was not deserving of resentment. If anything, knowing him had given her a glimmer of hope that she might someday overcome the reservations which continued to govern her.

Unshed tears gathered in her eyes and blurred the image of the wooded coastline. What kind of a Christian was she when it was her fondest wish that Ramsey Tucker was presently burning in Hades? God might have removed him from her life but He had not provided the strength to forgive. Without divine help, Charity knew she would always hate her late husband with a vengeance that made her literally ill.

Did she *want* to forgive him? she asked herself. Or was she purposely dwelling on the sordid memories of him to reinforce her loathing and keep from having to go on with life in a normal manner?

She scowled. For the first time in years she was starting to question her motives, her abject hatred. The conviction that that doubt brought with it was hard to accept.

It was far easier to continue to hate, she realized, than it was to consider putting her sad past behind her. Assuming she actually wanted to, was it possible? Did she want to try? Surely not.

Charity closed her eyes and thought of parts of

the prayer her mother had taught her so long ago. "And forgive us our trespasses as we forgive those who trespass against us," she whispered. That was the key, wasn't it? And that was exactly what she was *not* doing.

"But he hurt me so," she murmured, her words lost on the sea wind, tears beginning to slide down her cheeks.

Still standing next to her, Naomi reached out and gently patted Charity's hand. The gesture was fleeting and without explanation, yet Charity felt as if it were a sign from God, as if He were saying to her, "Now you see. Now you can begin to heal."

The sensation of peace and tranquility was so unexpected Charity's knees nearly buckled. She grabbed the railing and held on tightly. A peek at Naomi showed no change in her blank expression, yet apparently the Lord had used her to convey His support.

Awed and ashamed, Charity stopped trying to contain her tears and let them flow freely. As they fell, she felt as if they were cleansing her all the way to her soul.

She was sniffling, regaining control of her raw emotions and preparing to escort Naomi inside when the other woman turned, embraced her tenderly and began to pat her on the back the way a mother would comfort a distressed child.

"Don't be sad," Naomi said. "God loves you. My mama says so."

If Charity could have found her voice to answer at that moment she would not have known what else to add.

The enormous mouth of the Columbia was crowded with ships and boats of all sizes and shapes, including rustic dugout canoes, some large enough to transport dozens of blanket-wrapped Indians all at once.

Charity had heard of Indian canoes, of course, but had never dreamed any were so large and imposing. To her surprise and relief, the canoe riders seemed more interested in selling or trading fish, fowl and baskets full of fresh oysters than in causing mayhem or injury. Their shouts for attention were mostly in an unfamiliar tongue but judging by the way they were gesturing and displaying their wares, Charity had no doubt of their aims.

Beside her, Thorne pointed to the shoreline. "There's Astoria. See it? We'll change boats and proceed up the Columbia River to the Cowlitz before we start out overland."

"I understand your wish for haste," she said, "but wouldn't it be easier to continue on this steamer and take the coastal route all the way to Puget Sound?"

"Easier, perhaps," Thorne said soberly. "Not necessarily wise. We already know we have at least one enemy on board, maybe more. The sooner we thin the crowd and start to travel alone, the safer we'll be."

"That is a valid point," Charity said with a nod. "I was talking with one of the other women passengers, a Mrs. Yantis, whose husband owns a sawmill up in Olympia. She told me how much more tedious the journey by sea can be."

"You didn't reveal anything about us or our plans, did you?"

"Of course not." Charity gave him her best scowl. "I had to physically drag Naomi away from the conversation because she kept wanting to tell the woman about her missionary parents, though. I assume that's the kind of careless talk you were referring to?"

"Among other things. Once we reach land we may as well resume the use of our real names." A wry smile began to lift one corner of his mouth as he said, "I keep forgetting whether I'm supposed to be a Smith or a Jones, anyway."

Charity laughed lightly. "I know what you mean. I haven't concealed my last name but it is hard to remember how to address you and the rest of your family."

She sobered. "I suppose we're only fooling ourselves, since someone obviously already knows who you, Jacob and Naomi really are."

"Or they wouldn't have tried to harm her? You're right. Subterfuge seems pretty useless at this point."

"You know," Charity said, pursing her lips and striking the pose of a thinker, "it seems to me that our trouble has followed us from San Francisco. Therefore, I have to also assume that whoever is causing the grief must have come from there, too."

"Only if you also assume that our nemesis followed me and Aaron's family from New York harbor, and that's impossible. The *Gray Feather* carried no other passengers and was already fully manned. I would have known immediately if there were strangers on board."

"Oh. I hadn't thought of that."

Thorne nodded slowly, pensively, and drew his thumb and fingers along his jaw to the point of his chin as if smoothing a nonexistent beard. "There is no place on earth that Louis Ashton's influence and wealth cannot reach to cause harm. No city or territory that's too far or too remote. That's the main reason I want to start overland as soon as it's feasible."

"It seems odd that a seaman such as you would be so eager to start walking."

Thorne smiled at her. "I have no plans to walk. We'll ride horses when we have to and employ small boats as much as possible, including hiring Indian canoes, if you and Naomi have no objections."

Her eyes widened and her hand went to her throat in a natural gesture of self-protection. "Oh, dear. Are you sure that's safe?"

"I won't do it if I'm not assured so by local people. Captain Nash is convinced these Indians on the Columbia are friendly but I want more than one man's word on it. I'll go ashore in Astoria and see about immediate passage up the river as far as Rainier. From there we'll follow the Cowlitz, as I said."

"What about provisions. If I need to start cooking I shall need proper equipment and foodstuffs."

She glanced at the Indian canoes, reluctant to buy from them when there was such a serious language barrier.

"There's supposed to be a good merchant at Rainier. We'll either get what we need from him or from the store up the river at Cowlitz landing. Don't worry. I told you I have this all planned out."

"So, I see." She had to smile to herself at Thorne's overconfident attitude. Although he was cautious and thoughtful to a fault, she knew that the slightest change of circumstance could upset his well-laid plans like a bushel of apples in the bed of a runaway wagon. She had been through enough trials, experienced enough surprises, good and bad, to know that man's plans in the face of nature and providence were often laughable.

They had already weathered storms at sea and had coped with Naomi's continuing illness. Whatever was to come was unknown and might easily negate any sensible choices they made at present.

Charity looked to Thorne, smiled and said, "I am in your hands, sir. Whatever you feel is best for us, I shall endeavor to accept with grace."

He laughed. "I'll be holding you to that vow, Miss Beal. I sincerely hope you don't come to regret it."

Returning his grin she said, "So, do I, Mr. Blackwell. So, do I."

Chapter Twelve

Thorne found, to his relief, that the captains of the steamers plying the Columbia were a close-knit fraternity, prone to good-natured rivalry. Thus, he was able to procure passage for his party at a more than fair rate with immediate departure promised.

In reality, the *Multnomah,* another side-wheeler, remained in port at Astoria hours longer than he had been told it would and Thorne was getting more and more testy.

"This boat is bound for Portland but we'll disembark long before then," he told Charity and the others as he paced the small private space they had been assigned.

"Good." Charity eyed the pouting child seated on the floor. "Jacob is as restless as you are. I was hoping for a little time ashore. Are you sure we can't do just a tiny bit of exploring?"

"I'm afraid not. I was watching the dock area a few minutes ago and I saw Cyrus Satterfield climbing the hill toward Astoria. It's a very small settlement. I see no reason to tempt fate by joining him. Now that he's gone, our troubles may be over."

"You must be joking."

"No. Not at all. Satterfield is not continuing up-river with us so I see no more problems."

"Not from him, maybe," Charity countered. "That's assuming he was responsible for sneaking into our cabin, as you initially thought. We have no proof of his guilt one way or the other."

"Meaning, I may have been wrong? I doubt it. My skills for judging people are well-honed. Satterfield was up to no good. I'm certain of it." He could tell by the dubious look on Charity's face that she remained unconvinced.

"I suspect you may have been a tiny bit jealous of his interest in Naomi," she ventured with a wry smile.

"What? Don't be ridiculous."

Although she looked away rather than rebut his declaration of innocence, Thorne remained bothered by her suggestion. Surely, that could not be the case. Yes, he cared what happened to his brother's family but that was simply because he owed such an emotional debt to Aaron, alive or dead.

Examining his innermost heart, Thorne found no trace of lingering affection for Naomi. On the contrary. He wasn't deliberately placing blame for her presently unstable condition, but he did suspect that her own guilt over her prior maltreatment of her husband was at least partially responsible.

What he wanted most to do was continue the present discussion with Charity and explain exactly how he felt about the other woman. Since all of them were together in the cramped cabin that would be impossible, of course.

Further considering the constraint, he began to view it as advantageous. There were things—personal things—he was tempted to say to Charity that *must* remain unvoiced, at least until they had reached their destination in Washington Territory.

After that, perhaps he would consider speaking of his serious intentions. It had been years since he had entertained such notions toward any woman and he knew he should proceed with caution, especially in Charity's case. There had been times, when they had inadvertently touched, that he had glimpsed something akin to fear in her eyes and it had cut him to the quick.

Above all, he would strive to make sure she trusted him fully and was assured he would never cause her harm or pain of any kind. The best way to do that, he reasoned, was by example. He didn't know where his opportunities might lie but he was certain they would arise as they followed the trail north. And when they did, he would be ready to take advantage of them.

He just hoped and prayed that Miss Charity Beal would be open to accepting his sincere efforts to win her confidence and then, perhaps, her heart.

And if he failed? What then?

Thorne gritted his teeth and squared his shoulders

as he pictured having to bid her a final farewell. He didn't even want to contemplate such an utterly intolerable event.

Gazing at her as she played with Jacob, he realized that bidding either of them goodbye was going to tear his heart out.

Cyrus Satterfield had walked slowly away from the dock to make sure his entrance into Astoria was plainly visible. He wasn't going to try to follow Blackwell and his party too closely from here on out. He'd had his fill of encountering the taciturn seaman and trying to keep from laughing in his face. Besides, it wasn't brawn that would win the day, it was brains.

The first order of business was refilling his pockets with enough coin to buy his way through whatever snags he might encounter in the wilderness. Ashton had already supplied him with a generous stake and would have added to it in a heartbeat, he knew, if he'd had access to quick communication. As things stood, however, Cyrus figured he'd be lucky to keep up with his quarry even if he didn't wait around for more traveling money to arrive.

He sauntered into the first saloon he came to and bellied up to the bar. "Whiskey. And none of that rotgut you palm off on the Indians. Understand?"

"Yes, sir."

Purposely paying the bartender more than the drink was worth he gave him a conspiratorial smile and leaned closer to say, "I'm looking for a high-stakes game of chance. Any idea where I might find one?"

The man cocked his head toward a doorway in the rear. It was covered by a dirty, tattered, gray blanket nailed to the top of the frame rather than having an actual wooden door.

"In there?" Satterfield asked, incredulous.

"If you're up to it. They don't take no guff off'n strangers. You'd best have the wherewithal to play or they'll run you out of town. Or worse, if you get my drift."

"I fully understand," Satterfield said, picking up his drink and starting to turn away. "This shouldn't take long."

"Don't underestimate those fellas," the bartender warned. "They take their game very serious."

"I take everything seriously," the assassin replied with a snide smile. He paused. "Tell me, how much would it cost for you to get somebody to go down to the docks and delay the departure of a certain river-boat for an hour or two?"

Charity had managed to keep her small charge busy by sitting on the floor with him and teaching him to tie knots in the fringe on a lap robe she'd found in their new quarters. He was becoming very accomplished at the knots and she was kept well-occupied untying them so he could try again and again.

Thorne had gone out on deck long ago. She was beginning to wonder what had become of him when he reappeared to announce, "They're casting off. Finally."

"Good. No more sign of that man you were worried about?"

"No. None. Thank God." As he spoke he looked heavenward and Charity knew his thanks were being properly delivered.

"Then we can relax." She could tell by the look on Thorne's face that he didn't agree so she asked, "Well, why not? Surely we're safe on this little boat."

"From my stepfather's perfidy, perhaps," Thorne said. "But there are other dangers ahead."

"I thought you trusted God to look out for you. You once said you believed He knew our future. Have you changed your mind?"

"No." He offered his hand as she attempted to gracefully rise.

Since the boat was now in motion, Charity accepted his assistance rather than chance tripping on her skirt or voluminous petticoats. There were times, like now, when she envied the ease of men's movements, unhindered by all the cloth that fashionable women carried about on their persons. Her sister, Faith, still had the buckskin dress a Cheyenne woman had given her and was forever praising its comfort and simplicity.

"Thank you," Charity said, using both hands to smooth her skirt as soon as she got her balance. "How long do you expect this leg of our journey to take?"

"Probably several days, particularly because

we'll be fighting the current. In this case I highly recommend that you do take in the sights. The gorge is quite amazing, especially if you haven't seen it before."

"Oh, that's wonderful news! I do so prefer to be outdoors." She noted that he was beginning to smile at her and supposed he was amused by her childish enthusiasm. Well, that couldn't be helped. She'd been a virtual prisoner on the *Grand Republic* for over a week and had lived a terribly sheltered life at the hotel before that. Standing on deck to enjoy the unspoiled beauty of the wild lands on both sides of the immense river would be akin to being released from jail and transported straight to the Garden of Eden.

"I would have thought that a lady like you would have preferred a drawing room to the windy deck of a riverboat."

"Then you do not know me nearly as well as you think you do," Charity countered, also smiling. "I may once have been a delicate, shrinking violet but life has made me far more sturdy than that."

"Are you saying that some of your experiences were good for you?"

She laughed. "I wouldn't go quite that far. Suffice it to say that I have learned how to appreciate that which I do have and to waste less time coveting that which I do not."

"Such as?"

"I think this conversation has gone far enough, sir," she said, continuing to smile demurely. "Would you be so kind as to watch Jacob so I may take a turn around the deck?"

"Alone? Shouldn't I accompany you?"

"If you feel you must," Charity said honestly, hoping he would understand her need for time to contemplate, to soak up the wonders of the scenery without distraction. "Truth to tell, I covet a bit of peace and quiet." Eyeing the child she felt a pang of motherly love. "I do enjoy our little man but there are times…"

"Say no more." Thorne lifted the child in his arms and carried him to the door so he could open it for Charity. "You'd best wear the heavy coat. It's always windy here and as soon as we sail into the depths of the gorge the sunlight will be blocked by the high cliffs. You'll be easily chilled."

Although she took his advice before heading outside, she made no comment. It was comforting to have someone looking after her but she had been the caregiver for others for so long the shift in responsibilities was a tad hard to accept.

The man means well, she decided as she drew the heavy overcoat more tightly around her slim figure and leaned against the carved, white-painted, wooden railing at the leading edge of the uppermost deck. Thorne Blackwell had obviously appointed himself everyone's caretaker and took that job very seriously. There was nothing wrong with that. She was simply unwilling to surrender totally to his will. He wasn't a bit like her late husband had been, yet the notion of giving up her personage by subjecting it to his, went against the grain.

Charity stood facing into the wind to let the loose curls blow back from her forehead and cheeks, mindless of the damage to her carefully coiffed, upswept hair. She knew she should return to the cabin and fetch her bonnet but she couldn't tear herself away from the wonders before her.

Cliffs adorned with stately pines rose high on both side of the gorge, painting the rocky cliffs with patches of verdant green. Where there were narrow rifts she could often glimpse slim, towering waterfalls that looked as if they had turned to mist by the time they finally reached the base of the cliffs. From there they added their icy drops to the multitude of creeks and rivulets flowing into the mighty Columbia.

Seabirds mingled with eagles and other soaring, diving denizens of the canyon, sharing the air and the forest while calling to each other above the steady march of boats plying the waterway. Deer occasionally peeked out from the greenery, as did smaller creatures indigenous to the woodlands that had so recently been divided into Oregon and Washington territories by the American congress.

Unlike her, the wild animals clearly knew where they belonged, Charity mused. What was it the Bible said? *Don't worry about anything. If God takes care of the birds of the air and the lilies of the fields, you must see that He will also take care of you.*

Oh, how much easier life would be if only she

believed that the way Thorne did. She wanted to. Really, she did. Continuing to watch the passing scene, she grew melancholy. Perhaps someday she would find her place in the world, a place where she *knew* she belonged. A place where there was peace and love and acceptance. Home.

Thoughtful, pensive, she happened to glance at the shoreline on her left. At least five Indian dugout canoes were beached there and riders on horses and mules had formed into a group as they trailed their way up from the water on a narrow path that looked as if it followed the course of the river for a short way.

She stiffened. Frowned. Shaded her eyes and strained to see more clearly. Could her imagination be playing tricks on her or did one of those men on horseback closely resemble the man from the hotel whose presence had so vexed Thorne? She had only seen Cyrus Satterfield briefly since they'd left San Francisco, and then only from a distance, but this rider's clothing matched the details stored in her memory. Moreover, he stood out from the others because he wasn't dressed like a settler or an Indian.

There was only one way to find out. Lifting her hem and racing for the cabin, she went to fetch Thorne.

Charity's abrupt arrival startled Thorne and brought him to his feet. "What is it? What's wrong?"

"I—I think I saw him. That man. The one you were watching," she blurted breathlessly.

"Where?" He immediately usurped her position at

the door, blocked the entrance with his body and scanned the nearby deck area. "Did he bother you?"

"No, no," she explained. "It was on shore. I think I saw him on the riverbank with some Indians."

"Which shore? North or south?"

"I don't know." She glanced at the sky. "It's too near noon to tell."

Thorne did his best to temper his consternation. "We're headed almost due east. From the bow, north is to the left and south is…"

"North," she nearly shouted. "He was on the north shore."

"Stay here with Naomi and the boy. I'll go have a look," he called over his shoulder, already hurrying away.

In the seconds it took him to round the pilothouse and reach the port deck he prayed he'd be in time to see for himself.

He wasn't. The breath whooshed out of him in disgust. The riders Charity had spotted were still on the hillside but they were already too far away to be seen clearly, let alone identified.

Racking his brain, it suddenly occurred to Thorne to duck into the pilothouse and see if the captain had a spyglass handy.

He knocked but didn't pause before opening the door. "Excuse me," he said, quickly scanning the small room. "I was wondering if…"

The copper, cylindrical device Thorne sought hung in its leather case, just to the right of the doorway. He snatched it and was already back at the railing by the time shouts followed him.

Someone grabbed his shoulder, tried to wrest the spyglass from his grasp. He twisted away with a strong, "Wait! Just one more second."

"You can't go takin' the cap'n's property," the crew member said.

"I know. I'm sorry. I didn't have time to ask his permission. I needed to use it right away."

"Well, you've used it," the man countered. "Now, give it back or I'll have to place you in irons for the rest of the trip."

Thorne knew there was no use arguing further. He'd seen enough through the telescopic device to know that the riders were too far away for anyone to discern their features, even magnified.

He handed over the instrument and walked away without any comment other than a murmured, "Sorry." And sorry he was. If Charity had been right in her assumption that Cyrus Satterfield or others of his ilk were headed in the same direction as his party, they'd better be more vigilant than ever.

And if he wasn't? If Charity had been mistaken? That didn't change anything. As he had already told her, there could still be new dangers around every bend of the river and lurking behind every tree. Whether or not they were in real peril didn't matter. Thorne intended to proceed as if they were still centered in the sights of an invisible rifle and Louis Ashton's finger was poised on the trigger.

Chapter Thirteen

The steamer *Multnomah* put ashore near Rainier, a meager assemblage of rough-hewn buildings at the confluence of the Columbia and the Cowlitz. From there, Charity had been told, they would go as far as possible on the smaller river before undertaking a short, overland trek, passing through Olympia and proceeding to the American Fort Steilacoom.

It sounded too easy, which was partly why she was worried. The trip across the great plains by wagon had been described as simple, too, and it had cost many thousands of pioneers their lives. If accident or Indian attack didn't kill you, cholera or smallpox might, providing you didn't get run over by a wagon or a buffalo stampede or die of starvation and thirst, first.

And speaking of Indians. Charity shivered. Thorne had been talking with four long-haired, buckskin-clad natives while she and Naomi stood aside with Jacob. From the satisfied look on Thorne's face as he returned to them, she feared he had struck a bargain for their transport upriver.

"All's well," Thorne said. "One of their party is an important leader of the peaceful Nisquallies, so we're in good company. He tells me there are halfway houses all the way to Cowlitz landing where we'll be able to buy horses and supplies for the last leg of our journey."

Grinning, he gestured toward the waiting Indians. "Smile, ladies. We don't want Leschi and his friends to think you're unhappy. They've kindly offered to let us ride along on their trip home. We'll be departing as soon as they're through trading at the mercantile."

Naomi pressed a lace-edged handkerchief to her face below her nose, peered at the canoes and grimaced. "Those boats smell."

"That, they do," Thorne said. "And so do our friends if you judge them by our standards. I'm sure we smell very strange to them, too, and probably just as distasteful."

Charity nodded. "That's what my sister said after she and her husband had spent some time with the Cheyenne and Arapaho. She got so used to the aromas in camp she missed them after she left."

"I feel the same about the ocean," Thorne said, looking a bit wistful. "There is something about breathing sea air that invigorates and blesses me."

"Me, too," Jacob piped up, bringing chuckles from Charity and his uncle.

"Well, I guess we know where our little sailor's

loyalties lie," Charity said. "I was pleasantly surprised by how well he handled the bad weather that put his mama to bed. Thankfully, he seems to take after your side of the family."

Thorne's response was perplexing. She had thought, since he seemed so taken with the little boy, he would be flattered by the comparison. Instead, he was acting as if that was the last thing he'd wanted to hear.

He was probably still grieving over the possible loss of his brother, she reasoned. That excused his rigid posture and closed expression. It had been insensitive of her to bring up the subject and although she was sorry to have done so, she felt it best to let the matter drop rather than apologize and draw more attention to her innocent faux pas.

"Will we all be able to fit into one canoe with our baggage?" she asked.

Thorne shook his head. "No. We'll ride with Leschi and one of his companions. The others will transport our bags in the second canoe. The Nisquallies came downriver together and that's the way they plan on going home." He gave her a lopsided smile. "Consider it your own private fleet."

"I think I'd prefer something a bit larger for my armada," Charity said, relieved to have distracted him so easily. "But I imagine it will be safer with more guides. I don't suppose there's any chance they might get lost, since they live here."

"Not likely," Thorne replied. "They don't use compass and sextant like ships at sea but they always seem just as sure of directions as the finest trained navigator."

"Undoubtedly a useful talent," she said with a shy smile. "I, on the other hand, used to get lost as soon as I stepped off Montgomery Street near the hotel. Papa loved to tease me about it."

"You will see him again," Thorne said soberly. "I promise."

She sighed. "They should be married by now." Looking into the distant forest, she let her mind's eye wander. "I know Annabelle wanted the wedding to be held at Mission Dolores because that's where Lola Montez was married to Mr. Hull last year. Papa wanted to use Trinity Church, instead. It will be interesting to see who won out."

"I doubt it matters in the eyes of God," Thorne ventured.

"I hope you're right. I haven't been able to bring myself to attend worship services in a church since I left Ohio. I know I should have, especially when Papa asked me to go with him, but it just didn't seem right without Mama."

"What about your own wedding? Where did that take place?"

Charity shook her head slowly, sadly. "In the middle of a desolate prairie just west of Fort Laramie. It's not a day I particularly take pleasure in remembering."

"Then forgive me for bringing it up."

She looked into his eyes and replied, "If you, too, will forgive me."

"For what? You've done nothing needful of forgiveness."

"Yes, I have. I reminded you of your brother when I mentioned Jacob's sailing abilities a few moments ago. I should have been more sensitive. I'm truly sorry."

"Ah, that," Thorne said with an audible sigh. "You mustn't blame yourself if I seemed out of sorts, Miss Beal. The error in judgment was not yours. It was mine."

Thorne helped both women into the first canoe, then handed Jacob to Charity. With a buckskin-clad Nisqually at either end of the narrow craft and the center space taken up by the ladies and the boy, he could quickly see it would be best if he followed in the second boat instead of climbing in with them.

"I'll ride with the luggage," Thorne said. "It makes no sense for all of us to cram in together when it's not necessary."

"But…"

Although Charity didn't finish her sentence, Thorne saw her eyeing the regal-looking Indian seated in the prow of the canoe. Leschi was taller than his companions and apparently spoke several languages, English among them, which was a definite plus. Yet Thorne could tell she didn't relish being separated from him and his rifle.

"I'll be right behind you," he said to reassure her. "It will be much easier for me to watch out for you if we're not so crowded." He smiled wryly. "You said you'd trust me. Remember?"

She gave him a contrite look. "I did, didn't I? My error."

That made Thorne laugh. The Indians joined in, thereby lifting everyone's spirits. They pushed off with Charity's canoe in the lead and Thorne jumped into the second narrow boat.

He didn't like sending the women on ahead and was adamant that his canoe keep pace with Leschi's. It took an extra payment to the owner of the second canoe, after departure, to ensure that that occurred.

Smiling to himself, Thorne appreciated the crafty way his Indian guide had arranged to squeeze another coin out of him. These Oregon and Washington natives might be uneducated by city standards but they were clearly far from foolish. They had learned to trade from the British of the Hudson's Bay Company and had quickly adapted to the advent of Americans, nick-naming them "Bostons," apparently in the mistaken belief that all such settlers hailed from Massachusetts.

The Nisqually knowledge of world geography might be lacking but the Indians' overall skill at plying the rivers and lakes was quite impressive, es-pecially to a man like him who had made a good living from the sea. He was not only awed with the way each guide handled the small dugouts, he was amazed at how well the canoes balanced as they slid through the water with barely a ripple.

Concentrating mostly on the boat bearing the

women and the child, Thorne nevertheless found time to ready a rifle he had purchased on the docks in Rainier. It was a muzzle-loader and had seen lots of hard action, judging by the looks of its scarred stock. It, and the derringer he had given Charity, would have to serve until he found something better and added to their armament.

His guides barely glanced at him as he poured a measure of powder down the barrel, added a wad and ball, and rammed it all home, waiting to place a cap below the hammer until he was ready to test fire it. Not wanting to discharge the rifle for nothing and perhaps startle the others, he laid it carefully aside.

Ahead, Charity had slipped off her bonnet and he could see sunlight glistening off her golden hair. Although she resembled Naomi in coloring and height, there was a warmth and vivacity to her personage that set her apart from the other woman the way a sunset highlighted an otherwise cloudy horizon. She was sunshine to Naomi's shade; roses in full, glorious bloom to the other woman's spent blossoms.

Thorne could tell by watching their Nisqually guides that the Indians were growing wary of something. They kept to the center of the Cowlitz and alternately scanned both banks. He knew they would spot any danger long before he did. What they would do to counter it, however, was another question.

Peering into the shadowy vegetation along the riverbanks, Thorne imagined a multitude of threats. Every crack of a twig, every splash of water, every cloud that passed across the sun and left dappled patterns on the ground, made him see adversaries where there were none.

Suddenly, a horse whinnied close by. Another answered. Thorne spun around just as a rifle fired from shore. The sharp sound echoed up the canyon on both sides of the river, masking its origin all too well.

A woman screamed.

To Thorne's horror, he knew the shriek came from Charity.

The moment she had realized what was happening, Charity had thrown herself over the child to protect him.

The Indian called Leschi shouted something to her but he spoke so rapidly she couldn't understand what he was saying. She did know, however, that he and his companion were paddling their canoe much faster and had veered sharply left.

She dared not raise her head for fear of another shot but did manage a quick peek over her shoulder. Naomi had apparently not been hit or even frightened because she was still sitting bolt upright.

Appalled, Charity commanded, "Get down!"

Naomi ignored her.

Charity reached for the other woman's coat and yanked, toppling her over and pulling her down so they were all lying bunched up below the thick, wooden sides of the dugout.

There was no way to tell if that would be enough

protection but Charity figured it was better than letting Naomi just sit there, frozen like a frightened deer waiting for slaughter.

Jacob began to whimper.

"It's okay, honey. We're okay," she crooned. "I'm sure Uncle Thorne will shoot back as soon as he can."

Whining, the little boy displayed his hand. There was blood on it!

Charity took one look, raised high enough to be sure their protector's canoe was following closely, and yelled, "Help!"

She returned to her prone position and cradled the child in her arms to cushion him. "Where is it. Where do you hurt?" she asked.

He pointed. To her.

"You have a owie."

"I do?" Charity touched her forehead and her fingertips came away smeared with crimson. She hadn't felt a thing at first but now that Jacob had called her attention to it, her forehead did smart a little.

The sensation of being shot was nothing at all like she had imagined it would be. She had thought she had merely banged her head on the canoe when she'd ducked, never dreaming that her scalp had actually been grazed by a bullet!

Relieved that Jacob was not injured, she smiled at him. "It's just a scratch. I'm sorry I got blood all over you, sweetheart."

Naomi raised her own head enough to glance at the others, took one look at the gory mess and fainted.

* * *

Leschi had his canoe beached and had herded its occupants into the forest for cover by the time Thorne caught up to them.

He made straight for Charity, dropped to one knee and grasped her free hand while she used the other to press a scrap of cloth to her forehead just above the hairline.

He was beside himself, almost afraid to articulate his feelings for fear of revealing the pain he felt at seeing her thus. Finally, he asked, "Are you badly hurt?"

"No. I'm sure it's just a scratch. I'm afraid I frightened Naomi and Jacob terribly, though."

Blinking back tears of relief he heaved a sigh. "You scared me enough for both of them. Who shot at you?"

"I don't know. I never saw a thing."

Thorne didn't want to leave her but there were details he had to know. He arose and turned to the Indians. "Did you see anything?"

"Boston men," Leschi answered. "And Snoqualmies. Patkanim. He bad medicine. Want war."

"Are you sure it was Bostons with him?"

The taciturn Indian nodded. "All King George men tillicums, like Dr. Tolmie. They not shoot at Leschi."

"Friends?" Thorne guessed. "You say they're your friends?"

"Yes. Friends. Boston men not tillicum." He frowned. "Except Charlie Eaton. He marry my daughter, Kalakala."

"Then surely they are your friends, too," Thorne said, hoping to be considered among them.

Leschi snorted derisively and turned to point at Charity. "Why shoot klootchman?"

"What? Oh, the woman? I don't know for sure but I have a good idea. I just don't understand what the Snoqualmies would have to do with all this."

Chuckling, Leschi looked at him as if he thought him daft. "Patkanim's men no need reason. They love to fight. Any Boston man with gun is enemy."

"Then why would they join forces with one?"

"For enough blankets or powder and ball, they will fight for any man. Even a Boston."

Mulling over what the wise Indian had said, Thorne fetched his things from the second canoe and returned to care for Charity. Her beautiful hair was matted and her frock probably ruined but that was of little consequence as long as she recovered.

He again knelt at her feet as he poured water from a canteen onto one of his clean shirts.

She resisted his ministrations. "You are not going to use that lovely shirt to clean my wound. It's a ridiculous waste. I won't permit it."

"Do you have a better idea?"

"Yes. I can take care of myself." Starting to rise she swayed slightly.

Thorne was immediately at her elbow to steady her. "So, you say. It looks otherwise to me, Miss Beal."

Still, she objected to his efforts. "I can dip water

from the river and use this scrap of my petticoat to stem the bleeding just as I have been."

"And be shot again for your trouble?" He raised an eyebrow. "I thought you were smarter than that."

"I'm smart enough to know that whoever took a potshot at us is probably long gone by now."

"I have to agree with that. However, I'd prefer to remain in hiding until our guides have checked to make sure."

"I couldn't help overhearing you talking to them. Is it true that it may have been hostile Indians who shot me?"

"Unfortunately. According to Leschi, they were in the company of Americans. They could have been after anything, including our supplies."

Or you women, he added to himself. There was plenty of intermarriage between the settlers of the Pacific Northwest and local women, such as Leschi's daughter. It was the pale, European-featured women that the country lacked and Thorne imagined that they'd be very valuable trade items if they were captured.

The concept gave him a sick feeling in the pit of his stomach. He had brought innocents to this wild territory and it was his sole responsibility to see to their welfare. No one was going to get past him to harm those women and that child as long as he had breath in his body.

And what if something happened to him?

Thunderstruck at the realization of his party's vulnerability, he left the canteen with Charity so she could finish washing up, then took the Nisqually leader aside to speak privately to him.

"I know I only paid you to take us as far as Olympia but I can see I should have asked for more. If something was to happen to me, how much more money would it take for you to promise to care for the women and get them as far as Puget Sound?"

"Hudson's Bay Company or Fort Steilacoom?"

"Preferably Steilacoom but either is fine as long as they're safe there."

"They be safe. I do."

Thorne started to reach into his pocket but Leschi stayed his hand. "No. You tell Bostons at fort that Leschi help you. Give big talk. Make them listen."

"All right." Thorne offered his hand and the two men shook on the bargain. "Why do you want to make such an impression on them? Surely, they know you're a leader of your tribe."

"They know. They make me swear in court against three of Patkanim's braves. Boston's hang them. Say murder."

"And you want me to assure them that you're a good friend to all sides. I see. You have my word."

In his sea travels Thorne had often noted the rivalry between the two factions of settlers in the Northwest. Those British who had founded the colonies for the fur trade were understandably upset about the change of legal boundaries and the necessity to vacate properties they had once laid claim to. But they had no choice. Their government had made a binding agreement. Oregon had been split off from Washington and was now a separate territory to the south, while part of the northern edge of Washington that encompassed the sound also fell within the aegis of the United States.

And, apparently, the local tribes had chosen up sides just as they had during the Revolutionary War seventy-five years before. While the British King George men and the Americans called Bostons quarreled about who owned what, the natives were the real losers. They had probably already ceded too much power to the interlopers and judging by past history they were going to someday find themselves treated as strangers, unwelcome in their own country, the land of their ancestors.

Thorne watched as Leschi spoke to his men, gesturing as he gave them orders. Two of them left immediately and faded into the forest as silently and easily if they were no more than puffs of smoke from a dying campfire.

Those Indians were a part of this wild land just as he was a part of the sea, Thorne reasoned. They belonged here. The territory was their mother and father, their home and their partner in life, providing all they needed for health and happiness. It was little wonder that they resisted the intruders, who were not only plundering their natural treasures but also destroying the good quality of life they had once enjoyed.

The Whitman massacre after the measles epidemic, which Aaron had cited, was but the tip of the iceberg.

Disease, against which the Indians had no defenses, had already decimated many tribes and would do so over and over again until they either attained immunity or were wiped off the face of the earth.

Thorne feared it would be the latter. Watching Leschi dispatching his men, he wondered if his new ally had any idea of the long-term danger his whole tribe faced. He strongly doubted it.

And speaking of danger… He set his jaw as he looked over at Charity. She was taking her injury well but that didn't negate its possible seriousness. He'd have to watch her closely for fever or other signs of related illness as a result of the cut, yet he had to thank God that she had not been hit squarely. An inch or two, either way, and the bullet would have entered her brain. Then, instead of arguing over the misuse of his shirt they'd be digging her grave alongside the river.

Nearly overcome at the thought of losing her, Thorne had to fight the burgeoning desire to take Charity in his arms and assure her that he would always care for her. Always love and cherish her.

Although he knew that doing so would be foolish and unseemly, he was right on the verge of acting on the impulse. Then the fat would be in the fire for sure, wouldn't it?

He sighed deeply, thoughtfully, and mustered his self-control. Was it fair for him to ask to court her? Was there a chance she might allow such a thing? Or was she still determined to remain single, as she had stated so forcefully in the past?

He didn't know. Nor was the question relevant at present. They had miles yet to travel and no one but God could guarantee that any of them would survive the trek.

Thorne briefly closed his eyes and prayed that his Heavenly Father would watch out for all his loved ones. Especially Charity Beal.

Chapter Fourteen

By day's end, Charity had developed a throbbing headache. Although she was resistant to doing so, she finally resorted to taking a few drops of the laudanum they had brought along to quiet Naomi.

When they put ashore at a landing where a half-way house awaited with meals and lodging, she was feeling a tad better but was nevertheless glad to leave the confining canoe and stretch her legs.

Thorne was already ashore and offered his hand as she prepared to step across. "Careful. The bank is slippery," he cautioned as she passed Jacob to him first.

"I shall have to remember to wear my heavy boots tomorrow," she said. She took his free hand and allowed him to assist her while he held the child in his other arm.

"How is your head?"

"Larger than it was this morning, I fear, but it will do. Leschi tells me his men found fresh prints of unshod horses but no sign of whoever shot at me."

Thorne scowled. "I cannot imagine who would do such a thing to you. Naomi, yes, if the scoundrel was one of Louis's hired killers, but not to you."

"I've been giving that some thought," Charity told him as the friendly Indians assisted Naomi ashore. "I had removed my bonnet but your sister-in-law had not. Perhaps the shooter mistook me for her. We are somewhat alike, same hair color, same size, and I was caring for Jacob. From a distance it would be a natural mistake."

Judging by the look of consternation on Thorne's face she was convinced he had not considered the similarity before now. Truthfully, if she had not had so much time to sit quietly and ponder during the trip upriver she might not have drawn that conclusion, either.

She saw him glancing around at the forest, the river and the lodge built of logs they were about to enter. It was as if he were seeing danger lurking behind every rock and tree and she felt sorry for him. It wasn't Thorne's fault that his brother had disappeared or that his stepfather was deranged, any more than it was his fault that Naomi had become mentally unbalanced recently.

Thorne was clearly assuming responsibility for all the tragedy that had befallen his family. It seemed so unjust. Necessary, under the circumstances, but nevertheless an unfair burden.

She took Jacob from him as he herded everyone toward the place the Indians had called, "Hard-bread's", presumably because their meals were rumored to consist of mostly boiled salmon and hardtack. The medicinal, dulling effects of the laudanum were beginning to wear off and she was starting to realize how hungry she was.

Welcoming aromas of cooked food greeted her, wafting on the air from the open doors and windows of the cabin. If it hadn't been for the clouds of mosquitoes and biting gnats that also heralded their arrival she would have felt as comfortable there as in the dining room back at the Montgomery House Hotel.

Off to one side, Leschi and his men were pulling leaves from a fringe-leafed bush, crushing the foliage in their hands and rubbing it over their faces and exposed arms.

Charity smiled at the Nisqually leader and gestured with an unspoken query. To her delight he brought her a handful of the bruised leaves, which reminded her of tansy, and she was able to cover Jacob's face and hands with the juice before also using it on herself. The effect was marvelous. Not a single insect crossed the fragrant, spicy-smelling barrier.

"Thank you," Charity said, smiling.

The Indian bowed slightly, smiled, also, and backed away.

"Aren't they coming in to eat?" she asked Thorne.

"I don't imagine they're welcome," he said.

"Well, I never."

She passed the child back to Thorne and preceded him into the lodge. There were large bowls of steamed, pinkish fish and boiled potatoes on the plank tables. At the end of each stood an open wooden barrel filled with hardtack from which the travelers could apparently help themselves at will.

Without so much as a "by your leave," Charity hefted one of the bowls of cooked salmon, added a handful of hardtack and marched out the door with it.

She didn't look back, nor would she have stopped if anyone had commanded her to do so. Instead, she went straight to the Indians and presented the bowl to Leschi.

He tried to refuse but she persisted. "Are you hungry?"

He nodded.

"Is this food you like?"

Again, a nod.

"Then please take it, with our compliments," Charity said. "Mr. Blackwell will pay the innkeeper for it and you won't get in trouble. I promise."

"You are tillicum klootchman," Leschi said, formally accepting the bowl and holding it as if it were a precious gift. "When we reach Nisqually, I will give you a horse. You choose."

"No, no," she said, "I don't want to trade. This is no more than I would do if you were a guest in my home."

"And I would give you a horse or some other gift," he explained. "It is our way."

Astonished, Charity thanked him and rejoined her party. Thorne had obviously been hovering in the lodge doorway and had already made peace with their landlord over the purloined bowl of fish because no one looked askance at her as she reentered.

Just the same, she felt the need to explain. "I was simply trying to do the Christian thing and feed everyone fairly. However, it seems that is not the way things are done in this part of the country and I am now to become the proud owner of one of Leschi's horses when we reach his home. I sincerely hope we'll need one because I'm afraid it would be an insult to him if we turned it down."

The surprised expression on Thorne's face made her giggle. "I know what you're thinking. I was flabbergasted when he told me, too. But since he had already accepted the food, I didn't know what else to say."

The landlord, a squarish man with enough hair on his exposed forearms to make up for what his head lacked, spoke up. "You did good, lady. Real good. These here Indians don't take kindly to some of our ways and it would of been downright dangerous to refuse that there horse." He guffawed. "Wanna go take him some taters and see if you can git another one from him?"

"I did not feed those poor men for personal gain," Charity insisted. "I did it because it was right."

"Well, right or wrong," the landlord said, "Your instincts pro'bly saved your neck. If you're smart, you'll pick a nice horse when you get the chance, too. It'd be rude to choose an old, weak or lame one. Leschi and his tribe take special pride in their livestock. He'd be shamed in front of his people if you took a poor gift."

It struck Charity that the man was putting other words to the old saying, *Never look a gift horse in the mouth*. She said as much, bringing more laughter.

"That's right smart, ma'am. Besides, you don't need to check his teeth if'n you know horseflesh. Those Indian ponies can be tricky, though. Some old ones look about as good and strong as the younger ones do." He laughed again. "Kinda like them Indians out there."

"They're hardly animals," Charity said, taking no pains to hide her disgust at the man's inferences.

"Wait till you've lived around 'em some longer," he said. "They'll surprise you."

"The thing that surprises me," she began, before catching the look of warning in Thorne's eyes. There was no mistaking his admonition to quell her righteous temper.

She did the best she could to smooth over the situation by adding, "Forgive me for bothering you with my personal problems, sir. I'm weary and hungry and my head is throbbing." Giving the landlord a demure smile she asked, "May we sit down and eat?"

"Be my guest."

As they took their places on the narrow benches that bordered the longest sides of each table, Thorne leaned closer to whisper in her ear, "Thank you. I know that took considerable constraint."

"About all I could muster," she told him aside. "I fear I may have lived amongst city dwellers for too long."

Thorne shook his head. "Things are no different back in San Francisco."

"Of course they are."

"Oh, really?" He held the bowl of potatoes and helped her dish some out for herself and Jacob before he asked, "Then tell me. How many Chinese were lodged at the Montgomery House Hotel?"

Sleeping on the hard, wooden floor of the halfway house would not have been Charity's first choice of accommodations but under the circumstances she wasn't going to quibble.

The night had grown chilly as soon as the sun had sunk behind the surrounding hills and her place next to the hearth not only warmed her achy bones, it also helped keep more bugs away. Outside, the sounds of a forest twilight kept a steady cadence of chirping insects and frogs and the occasional hoot of an owl.

She curled her body around Jacob and cuddled him close so she could cover him with her heavy coat while he used her arm for a pillow.

It was easy to relax because she knew Thorne was sitting up, watching over them all. His presence was more than a comfort. It was a true blessing.

She wanted to thank him, to let him know how much she appreciated his evident concern over her injury and his efforts to care for her, but she didn't know how to do so without making her praise sound too intimate. If she were to reveal her feelings for him, she was certain he would be either astounded, offended or amused. Perhaps all of those.

In retrospect, she wondered if her initial decision to make this trip had been made for the wrong reasons. She had held Thorne Blackwell in high regard long before they had left San Francisco. And now? Now, her attachment to him was far stronger than simple friendship or admiration.

She lay quietly and listened to some of the men talking softly in the background. It was easy to pick out the familiar rumble of Thorne's voice, to know without peeking that he was vigilantly looking out for her. His concern was beyond any she had ever experienced and she wondered if he was that diligent and devoted to everyone.

Beginning to drift off to sleep, Charity smiled. It was pleasant to think that Thorne's allegiance was aimed toward her, as a person, rather than at the family as a whole.

Family? Yes, she answered, sensing a newfound inner peace. Somehow, she had begun to see herself as a real member of Thorne's immediate family and that view gave her great contentment.

She heard the muted clomp of boots approaching and opened her eyes. Thorne towered above her.

"I'm sorry to wake you," he said quietly.

"I wasn't asleep yet," she answered, drinking in the sight of his dear face. "Is anything wrong?"

"No. I just wanted to make sure you were feeling all right. No fever?"

"I don't think so." Charity yearned for him to bend down and touch her forehead. Before she could reason away her inappropriate desires she blurted, "Maybe you'd better see for yourself."

Thorne hesitated only seconds, then crouched and laid his hand on her brow. She closed her eyes, relishing the caress of his callused hand. All too soon he withdrew and stood.

"I think you're cool enough."

No thanks to your lovely, warm hand, she thought, blushing. What was wrong with her? She had never, as long as she could remember, felt anything like the longing she felt for this man. Had she drifted so far away from church that she'd become immoral?

No, Charity answered without hesitation. It wasn't wrong to dream of the kind of marital bliss her sister had found, nor was it a sin to fall in love.

That thought was enough to make her catch her breath. Was this what love felt like? Could she have been wrong to plan to lead a celibate life after she was widowed? Such a decision had seemed perfectly sensible at the time. Only now was it coming into question.

Her eyes searched the depths of Thorne's dark gaze. Was she imagining it simply because she wanted it to be so, or was there a new tenderness, a growing affinity in the way he was looking at her?

She was afraid to ask, afraid he would deny such emotions. Instead, she smiled and said, "Thank you for looking after me."

"I—I would like to…"

"Yes?" Her eyes widened. For the first time since she had known him, the commanding Mr. Blackwell seemed to be struggling to express himself.

"Nothing," he said flatly. "Go to sleep. We'll be rising early tomorrow so we can reach Cowlitz landing in one more day."

"Sleep well," she said tenderly, sweetly, willing him to know her innermost thoughts and sense her growing fondness for him.

Although he merely nodded, then turned away, Charity was positive she saw telltale moisture glistening in his eyes. In her heart of hearts she took that as an indication that he was becoming aware of her affection. That was a good sign. A very good sign.

She snaked her fingers out from under the heavy coat and gingerly touched her temple in secret as soon as Thorne had walked away. It smarted. A lot. And the skin beyond her hairline felt unusually warm. Speaking of signs, that one was *not* good.

Tomorrow, she would privately ask Leschi to recommend other medicinal plants to help her heal. She was not going to succumb to this wound—or to any other. Not when she was beginning to suspect she had so much to live for.

Their arrival the following evening at Cowlitz landing created quite a stir. It was only after the canoes had docked that Charity realized the furor was not because of her party, it was due to the presence of Leschi. Clearly, he was not only an important person among his people, he was revered.

She watched myriad blanket-wrapped Nisqually men and women gather around him as he made his way to a clearing located amidst a collection of square log houses which stood apart from the rest of the town's buildings. Every cabin in the group where Leschi had gone was exactly the same size and shape, leading her to conclude that this was the way the local Indians constructed their homes.

That was a surprise. She had listened raptly to Faith's vivid descriptions of the Arapaho and Cheyenne villages and their buffalo-hide-covered teepees so she had expected to see the same here. Obviously, the Nisqually stayed in one place long enough to build log houses.

As soon as Thorne had helped her and the others disembark, Charity asked, "Is this Leschi's home village?"

"I don't think so," he answered, speaking quietly. "But they do seem to respect him here so he's probably related. The Indians often intermarry to join their tribes in permanent alliances."

"Like the royal families of Europe?"

"Yes, now that you mention it. Exactly like that."

Thorne had lifted Jacob into his arms and seemed to be waiting for something so she stood quietly beside him until she ran out of patience. "Why are we just standing here? Can't we go into town and find a hotel?" She pointed. "I think I see several possibilities."

"You do. Our guides tell me a proprietor named Goodell offers excellent food and real beds. We'll spend one night at his hotel before we head for Olympia. But first I want to buy horses from our Indian friends."

"Is this where I'll be choosing the one Leschi promised me?"

"I'm not sure. All I know is, one will not be nearly sufficient." He glanced at her, then at Naomi. "I assume you can ride astride?"

"Of course. Faith and I used to hop on Father's favorite old mule, Ben, and trot him around the pasture all the time." She felt a blush rising to warm her already-flushed cheeks even more. "Of course, Mother didn't know we were doing it or she'd have pitched a fit."

"I hope Naomi is equally nimble because I'm not sure where I'd find a proper sidesaddle for her in an outpost as remote as this one."

"I'll be glad to teach her how to ride like a man," Charity said with a shy smile and a giggle. "We may not be graceful or totally modest, considering our long skirts, but we'll do. I promise."

"You are truly a marvel, Miss Beal," he said, grinning at her.

"In that case, I think you should begin calling me by my given name."

"That's not proper."

"If we were seated in a drawing room in San Francisco and sipping tea out of china cups I might agree with you. Out here in this wilderness, such formality seems a bit stiff and unnecessary, don't you think?"

"Will you call me Thorne?" He arched an eyebrow and gazed at her quizzically.

"If that is your wish."

He bowed slightly, clearly mindful of the child he was still holding. "It is, Miss Charity. And may I say it will please me greatly to hear my name on your lips."

That comment, along with his obvious good humor and the twinkle in his dark eyes, added even more color to her cheeks and she could feel the warmth spreading to her very soul.

"Then it shall be my pleasure." She hesitated, wondering how it would feel to actually speak his name aloud rather than merely think it. All she said in addition was, "Thorne," but she knew her tone bespoke a fondness for him that was unmistakable.

He sobered, nodded and whispered, "Charity."

The timbre of his voice gave her shivers and sent a tingle zinging along her spine. Never, in all her twenty years, had she heard anything that had thrilled and pleased her more.

"Did you get a look at her?" Cyrus Satterfield asked his Snoqualmie cohort.

"Ai. She is here. I see her with the man and the boy."

"A big man? Dressed in black?"

"Ai."

"All right. That's all I'll need you for. I'll finish this myself."

"No. I go with you."

Satterfield shook his head and gestured with his

lit cigar. "You'll do nothing of the kind. If you hadn't shot at that canoe, they wouldn't even know anybody was after them."

"You say kill pale woman. I do."

"No," Satterfield countered with evident rancor. "You didn't kill her. All you did was graze her with your musket ball or she wouldn't be walking around town this very minute."

"I kill next time," the brave insisted. "Put poison on ball like we do arrows."

That got Satterfield's attention. "Poison? You have such a thing?"

"Ai. Kill deer fast."

He noted the Snoqualmie brave's taciturn expression and didn't doubt that his own life would be in danger if he made an enemy of these Indians. "All right. You can stay with me. But only because I may need some of your poison and instruction on how to handle it. I don't want to accidentally hurt myself."

Nodding, the Indian turned and walked away, leaving him standing alone outside the saloon.

Satterfield muttered a few choice curses that referred to both the Snoqualmie's rotten attitude and a questionable parentage, then shrugged off the unspoken threat he'd glimpsed in the brave's eyes and entered the building. There was more money to be made before morning, before he would have to mount up and give chase once again.

In the meantime, he intended to enjoy himself to the utmost, even if the only whiskey he could get was rotgut and the only woman he could find to warm his bed was from a local tribe. He would have preferred one of the willowy blondes Blackwell had with him, but the short, squat Indian squaws would have to do. If he could find one that had not had her head bound as a baby, so much the better. Those sloping foreheads and elongated heads might be the Indians' idea of beauty but they turned his stomach.

Chapter Fifteen

The lodging he'd been able to obtain in Cowlitz landing was not as luxurious as Thorne would have liked for Charity and the others but it had sufficed. He had not been able to purchase everything they would need for the final leg of their journey, either, though he had been assured that one of the stores in Olympia would be able to furnish the rest of his gear.

Thanks to the needs of the lumbering operations nearby and the brisk fur trade, Olympia had sprung up on the banks of the upper Cowlitz between the river and a snaking finger of Puget Sound. All manner of freighting was being carried on there, both by river and via the sound. To his surprise, there was even a newly founded mail service operating by horseback and canoe between the town and the mouth of the Columbia, far to the south.

Thorne would have preferred to keep to the water as they had so far, but from here on it wasn't practical. According to information from the men who ran the mercantile, Rev. and Mrs. White had built their mission farm on the part of the prairie called Nisqually Flats, near Fort Steilacoom. Therefore, the fastest, best access to them was on horseback.

Leschi had wanted to tarry with his kinsmen at Cowlitz landing so Thorne and his party had proceeded without a guide. As they traveled in single file along the well-worn trail north toward Olympia and then Steilacoom, he kept a sharp eye out. He wished Leschi had seen fit to come along but he was thankful that the amiable Indian had at least explained the shortest, best route.

In spite of occasionally having to wade through swampland as deep as the bellies of their horses, Thorne and his party were making good time. They had encountered a startling number of cabins and small farms along the trail, many of which were occupied by American settlers. If they had stopped to visit with everyone who had invited them in, it could have taken weeks to finish the day-long ride.

Spotting a ramshackle, apparently abandoned dwelling just off the trail in a grove of trees, Thorne finally suggested they pause to rest and eat some of the food they had brought. If he had been making the journey alone, he would have pressed on but he could tell the women were tiring. Even Charity was starting to look unusually pale. Besides, the sky had darkened as if a storm were imminent and he didn't want them to be caught in the open if it started to pour.

"Oh, I'd love to get down," Charity said with a sigh of relief. "Jacob has been napping for the last hour or so and my arms are so tired they're tingling."

Thorne dismounted first, tied his horse's reins and the ropes from the pack animals' halters to nearby saplings, then laid his rifle and ammunition aside before he reached up to relieve her of the child. The weary boy barely stirred in his uncle's arms.

"Take him inside and see if you can find a good place for his nap," Charity said. "I can manage myself and Naomi."

"Are you certain?"

"Perfectly. These horses are small but I would still rather you did not watch us climbing down. We may not be as modest as we wish to be."

"All right. Just remember what Leschi told us about Indian ponies and get off on the right-hand side instead of the left. I'll only be a few steps away. As soon as I get Jacob settled I'll come back and see to the horses so you won't have to bother with them."

The land around the old cabin was overgrown and the place looked deserted. Nevertheless, Thorne knocked before entering.

The door swung open with a squeak, revealing a broken latch, as well as rusty hinges. Stepping inside, he noted a tinge of green moss on the flat surfaces of the rough-sawn furniture. Only the sagging and frayed ropes remained on the bed frames. Chipped, stained dishes were stacked on shelves against one wall. Pots and pans sat empty atop a small, black, wood-burning stove. The place looked as if its former occupants had simply given up homesteading and had walked away, leaving most of their belongings behind.

He shrugged out of his coat, spread it on the hard-packed dirt floor, then laid the sleepy child on it before starting back to assist the women and hurry them along. The sooner he got everyone to their final destination, the sooner the knots of nervousness in his stomach would ease.

Spotting another rifle standing in one corner of the single-room cabin, he delayed a moment longer to have a closer look at it.

Charity was loath to admit she was feeling worse by the hour. Hoping she could continue to mask her feverishness, she sat astride the brown-and-white-spotted mare Leschi had given her and watched Thorne until he was out of sight in the cabin.

Thunder rumbled in the distance. To her dismay, her mare and the other horses seemed to be becoming unduly nervous. Since she wasn't familiar with these small, compact, Indian ponies, she assumed it was their nature to be a bit high-strung and the impending storm probably didn't help their temperament.

She mustered her remaining resolve, ignored the throbbing of her head and started to dismount. Just as she swung her leg over the saddle, the horse sidestepped, almost causing her to fall. She kicked her right foot free, jumped and landed squarely on the mossy ground. The jarring of the landing made her already-pounding head feel as if it was about to explode.

"Easy, girl," she crooned, not letting go of the bridle for fear the mare would bolt. "Easy. It's just me. I know you're not used to all these petticoats flapping around but I can't help that."

With the reins looped around her hand, she grasped Naomi's horse's bridle and forced a smile. "Time to get down, dear. Do you remember how I taught you to do it?"

Naomi nodded but Charity could see that the woman was unsure.

"Just swing your left leg over and…"

Suddenly, a whooshing, snorting sound emanated from the forest behind them. It reminded her of the noise a startled deer made when it sensed danger.

Both horses reared back and rolled their eyes, whickering and blowing through flared nostrils. Charity held fast and tried to dig in her heels, but to no avail. She was being dragged along by the wiry animals as if she were as weightless as a feather.

"Naomi! Jump down. Now," she commanded. "Do as I say."

To her relief, that authoritative tone did the trick. Naomi alit with surprising grace and speed but to Charity's chagrin, that action spooked the horses even more.

Naomi's black-and-white mount pulled free first, wheeled, and headed for the wilds with its ears back and its tail held high. Both packhorses immediately jerked their lead ropes loose from the sapling they'd been tied to and gave chase amid more lightning and crashes of thunder.

Charity hung on to her little mare in spite of its determination to follow the others. Where was Thorne? Hadn't he heard the furor? She supposed not or he would have come running by now.

She was continuing to try to calm her mare when a war whoop echoed across the glade and made the hair on the back of her neck prickle.

Another more distant whoop answered from the opposite direction. She thought she glimpsed slight movement through the trees and brambles. Here and there she could catch glimpses of brown color similar to that of the Indian clothing she'd noted in Cowlitz and beyond.

No matter which tribe members had made that chilling noise, Charity knew that she and the others were going to be afoot if she didn't retain at least one horse. She was also convinced that standing out in the open was the worst place to be, especially because any friendly natives would surely have shown themselves by now.

"Naomi! Come on. Never mind the other horses. Help me get this one inside."

Tugging, cajoling and backing away, Charity managed to urge the mare all the way to the cabin door. What she wasn't able to do was convince the horse to step foot into the darker interior.

"Thorne," she shouted over her shoulder. "Help us!"

* * *

He wheeled in response to Charity's cry and saw her trying to coax one of the fractious, half-wild Indian ponies through the doorway.

It would have been laughable if she had not had such a distressed look on her face. "What in the world are you doing?"

"Indians," she blurted. "Outside. I'm sure I saw them sneaking through the woods and I was afraid they'd steal my horse."

"Where's Naomi?"

"Right behind me."

The mare had its head lowered, its ears laid back, its neck bowed and its feet set, giving Thorne plenty of room to peer over its back. He caught his breath. "Where?"

"Right out there. The other horses ran off but she's helping me get this one through the door."

Thorne was already shoving the balky animal out of the way, much to Charity's obvious consternation. He didn't care if he made her angry. He had more pressing concerns. He could see most of the clearing and there was not even a hint of his sister-in-law.

About to grab the lone remaining mount and race to Naomi's defense, he heard a musket boom. The ball hissed by, barely missing his head, and thudded into the log wall behind him.

Charity gasped, then dived for cover.

Thorne darted aside to grab his ammunition bag and his rifle from the ground where he had laid them.

Charity's frightened pony nearly ran him down as it reared, wheeled and fled.

There was nothing he could do but follow Charity back inside and slam the cabin door.

"I'm sorry," Charity said, fighting to appear calm and failing miserably. "Naomi was coming with me. I know she was."

When Thorne made no comment, she assumed he was angry. Well, he had no right to be. She had done all she could. It wasn't her fault that she had failed. She was only one woman with two hands. She couldn't possibly have held on to the horse and Naomi at the same time.

Disgusted with herself, she sighed. No, she couldn't have. And in that case she should have chosen to drag Naomi into the cabin and let the horse be stolen. She realized all that now, when it was too late to do things differently.

"What now?" she asked.

He pointed. "Grab that old long gun standing in the corner and check that there's nothing blocking the barrel. I'll show you how to load it. The powder and ball are over here by me. The caliber should be close enough. You can add extra wadding if the ball seems too loose."

"Papa taught me how to load a gun," she said. "But how do you know this one is safe? It might blow up when you fire it if it's been sitting here rusting for very long."

"We'll have to take that chance." Thorne poked the barrel of his muzzle-loader out through a chink in the logs and sighted along it, waiting for a target.

"Maybe they were just after the horses," she ventured.

"Well, they have them now. And all our supplies."

Although he hadn't added, "How could you let them get away?" it was implied.

"I did the best I could," Charity insisted. "I know I should have let the mare go and held on to Naomi. She was right there, supposedly helping me. I never dreamed she'd run off like the Indian ponies."

"Did you see any special markings or clothing on the men? Anything that would help identify them?"

"No. Nothing. The horses got all het up and the next thing I knew, they were heading for the hills. Literally."

As she spoke she was checking the abandoned long gun by measuring the barrel with the ramrod to make sure there was no powder or ball already taking up space in it.

"This one isn't loaded," she said. "The rod goes in all the way to the percussion hole. Do you want me to load it for you?"

Thorne nodded. "Yes. Keep the first measure of powder on the light side till we see how it shoots."

She watched him sight his own rifle, hold his breath, then squeeze the trigger.

The gun went off with a boom that rattled the rafters and brought a shower of dust down on them to mingle with the cloud of pungent smoke from the burned gunpowder.

Jacob began to wail.

Charity was too busy to tend to him but she did call, "It's all right, sweetheart. Stay where you are. Uncle Thorne is taking care of us."

He passed her the first rifle to reload and took up the second one. "Wish me luck," he said, raising the stock to his shoulder and preparing to shoot again.

Charity chose to pray instead. *Father, help him. Help us. And please keep Naomi safe, wherever she's gone.*

There were more unspoken words, more silent pleas, and she didn't stop praying hard until Thorne had pulled the trigger of the second gun and its breech had held.

If it hadn't, she knew all too well that he could have had the whole side of his head blown off. That kind of accident had happened to careless men more often than she liked to recall, whether the metal was faulty to start with or they had thoughtlessly filled the breech with too much black powder.

Thorne fired, again and again, and Charity kept him supplied with loaded weapons. As she tore more pieces of fabric from her petticoat to make patches for the musket balls, she wondered what they'd run out of first. It didn't really matter. Once any of the other components, powder, ball or primers were gone, they would be defenseless.

The firing ceased as abruptly as it had begun. Charity froze, staring at Thorne and trying to read his unspoken assessment of their situation. He looked a lot less worried now than he had before. That was definitely a good sign.

"Are they gone?" she asked, reeling from fatigue and the effects of the fever she continued to deny.

"It looks like it." He straightened and propped the guns against the wall. "Keep everything loaded. I'll go have a quick look around."

"Take a rifle. You have to have something for protection."

"You keep them," he said, his gaze locking with hers as if he might never see her again. "If any Indians come through this door, don't let them take you alive."

"Whoa," she blurted, stunned. "I'd rather be a live hostage than a dead memory. Besides, I know you'd rescue me, no matter how long it took."

"I would, you know."

Her voice gentled as she reached up to cup his cheek with her palm and said, "Yes, Thorne. I know you would."

Though he didn't reply with words, the look in his eyes spoke volumes.

It wasn't until Charity was alone that she allowed herself to plop onto a rickety chair. Every bone in her body ached and she feared she was becoming very ill. That wouldn't do. Not at all. She must hold herself together and feign good health, at least until they reached Naomi's parents. After that she could let down her guard and allow her weakness to show.

Timidly, his cheeks streaked with tears, Jacob approached her. His voice was barely audible as he said, "Mama?"

Charity opened her arms and lifted him onto her lap. What could she say? How could she explain to the child that his mother was gone again and that it was her fault?

As her own tears began to fall, Charity held him close and laid her cheek on the top of his head. She was so weary, so spent she could barely think, let alone speak coherently.

Finally, she managed to say, "I'm sorry, sweetheart. I'm so sorry."

The little boy's response was both touching and heartbreaking. He wiggled and twisted till he could wrap his arms around her neck, kissed her damp cheek and said, "It's okay, Mama. Please don't cry."

Thorne returned after spending only a few minutes outside. "It's me. Don't shoot," he called before easing open the door.

Charity didn't rise to welcome him back. She wanted to run straight into his arms, regardless of the impropriety of such an action, but she simply lacked the strength to do so.

Jacob, however, had plenty of energy to spare. He shouted, "Uncle Thorne!" and raced toward him.

Catching the child in midstride, Thorne lifted him and swung him in an arc, sharing his joy as he glanced over at Charity. "I'm glad one of you is happy to see me."

"I'm happy, too," she said. "Honest I am." Getting to her feet, she swayed as a wave of dizziness and nausea washed over her.

Thorne hurried to her side and took her arm to steady her while he lowered Jacob to the floor. He peered at her. "You've been crying."

"I guess I'm not as strong as I thought I was."

"You're amazing. Most women I know would have fainted dead away at the first sign of Indian attack."

She blinked, trying to clear her head, and failed. The room was spinning. Colored lights like the bits of sparkling glass in a kaleidoscope danced at the periphery of her vision. Blackness encroached.

She heard the rumble of Thorne's voice. It sounded so dim and far away she couldn't make out what he was saying.

One moment of peace. That was all she needed. She'd just close her eyes for a second and she'd be fine. She had to be. Failing to hold up her end of the bargain she'd made to care for the dear little boy and his mother was totally unacceptable.

Moisture flooded her already misty vision and tears once again slid down her cheeks as she recalled Jacob's words. He had called her *Mama.*

The importance of that choice was not lost on her heart or mind and that was all she could think of as she slipped further and further into the darkness that was waiting to give her rest.

* * *

Thorne caught her as she swooned and carried her to where he had placed his coat for the boy. Laying her gently atop the garment, he knelt at her side and began to pat her hands and rub her wrists.

At his side, Jacob was sniffling. "Is she sick?"

Thorne was about to assure him that Charity was merely overtired when it occurred to him that the boy might be right. He hadn't felt her forehead since the night before and it was possible she might have chosen to hide her infirmity rather than cause more worry.

His hand was shaking as he gently laid it on her forehead. She was burning up! His anger flared. The little fool hadn't given any indication that she was ailing or he would never have asked so much of her. Did she expect him to notice her feverishness on his own? Or was she purposely hiding those telltale symptoms to keep from causing a delay in their journey?

Any and all of those possibilities fit Charity's stubborn personality, he concluded. The question now was what should he do? If he tried to carry her the rest of the way to Olympia, or at least as far as the next farmstead, they would most likely be attacked en route. If that happened while they were out in the open, there was no way he could adequately defend both her and the boy, let alone get her to a place where she could be nursed back to health.

He looked around the cabin, assessing his options. They were meager to say the least. If they stayed there, he would have to find fresh water and food, which meant leaving Jacob and Charity unguarded for however long that quest took.

If he chose to stay inside and continue to protect them, they might all fail to survive without adequate provisions, especially water. It was a terrible choice to have to make.

Finally, in desperation, he took his questions to God. As he knelt beside the unconscious woman and bereft little boy, he closed his eyes and began to mutter a prayer. His plea was mostly centered on Charity, on the fact that he truly cared for her, although he did include the rest of his close family, including Naomi and Aaron.

Unashamed, he released the strong self-control on which he prided himself and bared his soul to his Heavenly Father.

As a man, he knew was out of options and saw no way to save his beloved.

As a Christian, he knew upon Whom he must rely if any of them were to survive.

Chapter Sixteen

The storm that had been heralded by the thunder began in earnest before another hour had passed. Heavy rain pounded against the roof of the cabin and trickled in through a myriad of chinks between the logs.

Desperate for water of any kind, Thorne placed the empty cooking pots where they would collect rain while he tried to keep their guns and clothing dry.

He'd built a fire in the stove using some of the furniture for fuel and was applying damp compresses to Charity's fevered brow. She lay wrapped in his overcoat, as well as her own, while he tried to sweat the fever out of her. So far, his method seemed to be working because she had passed through a slight delirium and was beginning to rest easier.

Thorne knew he should stop worrying but he could barely manage to breathe, let alone relax. The only time he had left her side was to stoke the fire or collect more cool rainwater with which to bathe her face and hands.

Jacob, bless his heart, had tried to help by moving some of the smaller pans beneath newly discovered leaks and Thorne had encouraged his efforts. As long as the boy was kept busy he was less likely to notice undue hunger or thirst.

It wasn't until Thorne noticed him taking secretive sips of the collected water that he realized he'd had an ulterior motive. That made him smile in spite of everything. Jacob was a chip off the old block, all right, a conniver with a penchant for doing as he pleased, even at such a young age.

Thorne no longer doubted that he was the child's true father. There were simply too many indications of it. Not only did Jacob look enough like him at that age to have been his twin, he was displaying many of the same mannerisms and attitudes. Even his lopsided smile was pure Blackwell, leaving Thorne torn between pride and a sense of wretched culpability.

"If only Aaron were here," he said softly. "I have so much debt to repay."

He glanced at the leaky roof and thought of other debts, mainly the thanks he owed to God for providing needed water. It sounded as if the rain was slacking off, but they had plenty saved to get them through the night and hopefully bring Charity's fever down. Beyond that, he dared not plan. Without horses and the guarantee of a safe passage, he'd be a fool to try to complete their journey, no matter how close they were to Olympia or Nisqually Flats.

There was also the matter of what may have happened to Naomi. If the Indians had stolen her, he had to attempt a rescue or at least try to buy her back from them before she was bartered to some other tribe. The Indians' practice of slavery among their brethren had surprised him the first time he'd heard about it but it was such a big part of their warrior culture he knew he'd have to play by their rules. Assuming they did have Naomi, that is. If she had simply wandered off and had had to weather the storm alone and lost, that might be even worse.

Jacob had laid himself down beside Charity when he tired and had quickly dropped off to sleep. Thorne had kept the fire going as he stood watch. Hour by hour, his fatigue grew. His eyelids felt leaden, his alertness nearly nil. He fought sleep rather then allow himself much-needed rest. He must not doze, he insisted. If he wasn't vigilant, anyone could sneak up on them.

Finally, he decided to hang some small tin cups above the closed door so they would clatter and rouse him if it was opened. Then he sat down on the dirt floor with his back to the wall and the rifles at hand.

In minutes after he'd rigged the alarm and settled his weary body comfortably, he nodded off.

Charity awoke to sunlight streaming through the cracks in the walls and ceiling. She was still a bit achy but her headache was gone and she could tell the fever had also passed.

"Praise God," she whispered as she left the still-sleeping child and got slowly, tenuously to her feet to check her balance. Thankfully, she seemed to be a bit weak but otherwise as well as could be expected. She didn't remember everything that had occurred the previous day but she did recall enough bits and pieces of it to realize that Thorne had nursed her through the crisis.

And sweet little Jacob had helped, she added. How hard and how sad it was going to be to bid that child farewell.

Looking around the room she saw Thorne dozing in a seated position on the hard-packed floor. His coat was still on the ground where he had laid it for her and the boy and she knew he must be chilly, yet he was obviously sound asleep in spite of any discomfort.

Her mouth was dry, her throat parched. She found a pail of clean water with a dipper near the stove and slaked her thirst. Never had tepid water tasted so wonderful. The only thing better would be a bath. That was out of the question under these circumstances, of course, but she could clearly imagine its refreshing qualities.

She gently touched her wounded forehead. The place where the bullet had broken the skin was still tender but the surrounding skin felt cool, probably thanks in part to the pine bark Leschi had shown her how to steep and apply, as well as drink. That medicine was gone now, as was everything she owned, including her comb and brush, which meant that there wasn't a thing she could do to make herself more presentable.

If she hadn't been so glad to be alive, she might have fussed more. As it was, she knew there were far more important concerns to address, Naomi among them.

Thorne looked so peaceful, so dear, she yearned to let him sleep. Perhaps, if she eased open the door, she could make a silent trip to the facility out back and return without disturbing him. Since there didn't seem to be any other choice, she felt justified in doing so.

Charity didn't notice the tin cups balanced above the door until they clattered together.

Thorne was instantly awake. He jumped up, bracing for attack. When he saw who was standing at the door, he heaved a noisy sigh. "Oh, thank the Lord. How are you this morning?"

"Much better." She knew her smile was sheepish but she didn't care. She was so glad to hear his voice and look into his eyes she wouldn't have cared if he'd been yelling at her. "I was pretty sick, wasn't I?"

He nodded, his expression grave. "Yes."

"Thank you for taking such good care of me."

"I'm just glad my efforts were successful." Raking his hair back with his fingers he glanced at the floor where the boy slept. "Jacob's okay, too?"

"He seems fine. I'm sure my feverishness was due to the injury, not illness. I've never been shot before."

"And hopefully never will be again," Thorne said. "We should take whatever we think we'll need for the rest of our journey and get started as soon as possible, if you think you're up to it."

"I seem to be all right. I'm a little weak but not terribly dizzy the way I was." Reaching into the pocket of her coat, she withdrew a handful of crumbs. "I was going to offer you and Jacob some hardtack but I seem to have crushed it."

"You're the one who should eat it. You need to build up your strength."

Charity began to grin at him. "Are you being solicitous or is that your way of politely saying you don't want to share my crumbs?"

Laughing, he mirrored her broad smile. "I'm glad to see your sense of humor hasn't suffered. Don't throw that mess away till we get other food somewhere. We may end up eating it as a last resort."

Although she made a face she stuck her hand back into her pocket just the same. "All right. If you insist. I suppose it might not be too hard to take if we made it into a gruel. Where did you get all this fresh water?"

"The Lord sent it," Thorne said. "Right through the roof."

"I must have missed that."

"Undoubtedly. You were out of your head for hours."

Seeing affection and lingering concern in his eyes she wondered if she had babbled anything revealing during her delirium. She certainly hoped not. It was embarrassing enough to know that he—and Jacob, of course—had cared for her while she lay senseless.

If she had not trusted Thorne implicitly, she might have worried that he had taken advantage of her help-lessness the way Ramsey Tucker once had. But that was not even a mild concern. She *knew* Thorne would never hurt her, never abuse her in any way.

That startling realization was so firm, so clear, her jaw dropped. She stared at him. The fear of being touched, at least by the man who was looking back at her so lovingly, was totally gone. What a wonderment!

"Are you sure you're all right?" he asked, start-ing to scowl.

"Oh, mercy yes." Charity beamed. "I'm fine. Never better."

"Good." His eyes narrowed further. "I think."

"In time I will share my private thoughts with you but for now I agree that we'd best get a move on." She looked away and blushed slightly. "If you will kindly watch for hostile Indians, I would like to use the facility."

"Of course." Thorne picked up one of the rifles, opened the door a crack to check the yard, then threw it open as he said, "All clear. Follow me and stay close. I don't want you going into that outhouse until I make sure it's good and empty."

Charity knew better than to argue. She would have preferred to take care of necessities without causing such a fuss but she knew Thorne was right to be cautious, especially in light of the Indian attack the day before.

Without hesitation she followed him into the sunlit glade. Wildflowers, nourished by the rain, were blooming in clusters of blue and yellow at her feet while birds soared in the cloudless sky or busily built nests in the nearby trees. It seemed impossible that there could be danger lurking in such a beautiful place but she knew it was not only possible, it was probable.

She had no sooner left the cramped facility and rejoined Thorne in the yard than she saw an Indian step boldly into the clearing. Her breath caught. Her heart raced.

The instant the man raised his hand in greeting she recognized Leschi. Behind him, one of his men was leading the runaway horses. Looking slightly soggy and every bit as confused as ever, Naomi was once again seated atop the black-and-white mare.

Charity was confused, too. She'd trusted the Nisquallies, as had Thorne. Was it possible that they had been the ones who had fired on the cabin?

No, she countered. If they had been the attackers, Leschi and his men would be long gone, not smiling and returning their horses and property.

Tears of gratitude filled her eyes and prayers of thankfulness filled her heart.

She stood back as Thorne cautiously approached the Indian. She could hear the men talking but couldn't make out every word. When Thorne lowered his rifle and offered to shake Leschi's hand, her fears were allayed.

God had more than answered her prayers for their deliverance, she mused, elated. He had not only given them water when they were in dire need, He had provided native guides again to lead them the rest of the way through the wilderness. Their troubles were over.

Olympia wasn't a surprise to Thorne because he had sailed close to that portion of the territories often while navigating Puget Sound. Charity, on the other hand, was clearly impressed. He had to smile at her enthusiasm.

"Look! Real hotels, just like in San Francisco," she said, beaming. "And see that sign? It even has a newspaper, the *Columbian.* We must try to get one and see what's been happening while we were traveling."

Thorne laughed. "I doubt the news will be as fresh as we were privy to in San Francisco. It would have either come by the same route we did or been sent overland, probably from New York. Either way, it's a long trip, even with the new railroad lines that run partway."

"I suppose you're right. How many people do you think live here?"

"One or two hundred, I imagine. Judging by the piles of spars, shingles and squared timbers stacked down by the docks, the lumber mills are going strong.

There are undoubtedly a lot of folks living outside the city, too."

"Can we stay the night at one of the hotels?" Charity asked. "Our little man is badly in need of a bath. And so am I, I fear."

"You could have gone for a dip in any of the creeks we passed along the trail," Thorne teased.

"Brrr. You may be that hardy but the rest of us are not, I assure you. Besides, the sooner we reach Naomi's parents the happier I will be."

"Amen to that," Thorne said seriously. "Leschi is going across to the west side of the bay to stay with relatives tonight. He said he'd call for us at the Sylvester Hotel at dawn. That's the big log building at the corner of Main and Second." He pointed. "Right over there."

Leading the way, Thorne rode ahead, trusting Charity to herd Naomi in the right direction. He knew she'd been terribly distressed to have lost track of his sister-in-law, because ever since they'd gotten Naomi back, Charity had hardly taken her eyes off her.

"I'll see about rooms and stabling for the horses," Thorne said. He took special pains to smile as he added, "Can you handle Jacob and Naomi?"

"Jacob, yes," Charity said. "As for Naomi, I will give it my best."

"As you always have, even when you were so ill you could hardly stand. I want you to know I don't blame you for her foibles. She is what she is. All any of us can do is our best."

Tarrying, Thorne decided to help Charity down after he had dismounted. He held up his arms, took Jacob from her and stood him on a low stump that protruded from the edge of the street in front of the hotel. Then he returned for Charity.

"I can manage," she protested.

"I know you can. However, there is no way you can preserve your modesty if you err in the middle of this bustling settlement so you may as well give in and accept my assistance."

It was all he could do to keep from laughing at her expression of consternation. She knew he was right but she was still acting stubborn.

"Of course, if you want to try getting down by yourself, I can always stand back and watch," he added.

"I would rather you be close enough to cover my inelegance if I do show a bit of what's left of my poor petticoats," she replied, blushing. "I trust you will be enough of a gentleman to avoid staring."

"I shall be the soul of discretion," he vowed, chuckling as she leaned toward him and placed her hands on his shoulders.

She had already shed her heavy coat so he was able to grasp her thin waist. He lifted her easily, stepping back and sweeping her to the ground in one graceful swoop.

An instant later, as he lowered her feet to the dirt, he realized he'd made a terrible mistake. He never should have gotten that close to her again. She felt perfect in his arms, as light as a sunbeam and as beautiful as a butterfly. In contrast, he saw himself as clumsy and ill at ease. When he was this close to Charity Beal, he was no longer a shipping magnate or even an able seaman. He was an awkward boy longing for his first kiss from the woman of his dreams.

Ignoring the fondness he imagined in her lovely blue eyes, he set her away and quickly turned his attentions to helping Naomi.

From now on he would have to be even more diligent in regard to his actions, let alone his wayward thoughts. Charity was a lady of the highest order and deserved not only courtesy but honorable treatment. The more he grew to care for her, the more prudent he would have to be or he would surely alienate her.

Judging by the loathing she had demonstrated whenever she'd mentioned her late husband, he would have to be oh, so cautious. If he once stepped over the line and frightened her by making undue advances, no matter how gentle his approach, she might never be able to forgive him. Never be open to becoming a wife again.

When the right time came, when he was assured she would accept him, he would speak up and ask for her hand. Until then, he would keep his distance, for her sake and for the sake of their future happiness, even if the strain of biding his time was the hardest task he had ever undertaken—and he had little doubt that it would be.

Chapter Seventeen

True to his word, Leschi had appeared in the street outside the Sylvester Hotel at daybreak. Charity had already risen and seen to Jacob's immediate needs, as well as helping Naomi dress, so they were all ready to leave when Thorne called for them.

More time in the saddle did not particularly appeal to her but the weather was clear again and it felt good to soak up the sun's warmth as they rode Northeast across the rolling prairie.

By the time their mounted party reached the bluffs overlooking the place Leschi called Nisqually Flats, Charity understood why Naomi's parents and their neighbors had settled there.

The valley was a veritable Eden. Long, lush grasses waved like wheat in the cool breezes from the nearby ocean, and where there were cultivated patches of land she could see plots of healthy, farmed crops.

Charity had been balancing Jacob in front of her

on the wide tree of the saddle and pointing out squir-
rels, rabbits and other wildlife along the trail, much
to his delight.

When she reined in next to Thorne to gaze at the
valley below, she was in awe. "It's beautiful. Look
at all that grass. If Papa's old mule, Ben, were here,
he'd think he'd died and gone to heaven."

"This place is like that to the Nisquallies," Thorne
observed as their Indian guides left them with a part-
ing wave and proceeded down a separate trail toward
their own homes, as planned.

Thorne waited till Leschi and his tribesmen were a
little farther away, then explained, "All they need or
want comes right from the land. They tell me they har-
vest clams and oysters from the salt marshes, salmon
from the rivers, wild berries and other fruits in summer,
besides peas, potatoes and wheat from the tilled land."

"They're farmers? I had no idea. When I saw the
crops, I just assumed they belonged to the settlers."

"Some of them do. The Nisquallies have worked
for the British and Americans for years now and
they've learned how to raise their own crops, as well
as gathering the natural bounty from the sound and
the surrounding forest."

"That's amazing."

She continued to sit there and drink in the view
while Thorne scanned the trail behind them. Finally,
he said, "I think we should be going."

"Why?" She tensed and looked behind her. "Did
you see someone following us?"

"No. It's just a worrisome feeling I can't seem to shake. If there were any hostile Indians in this vicinity, I'm sure Leschi would have sensed it."

"Would he have said anything?" she asked, almost ashamed to be entertaining such suspicions.

"I think so," Thorne said. "But I understand what you're asking. I suppose it's not wise to trust anyone too much. If I were in the Nisquallies' moccasins I don't know how hospitable I'd be to hundreds of newcomers."

"Surely, there's enough bounty in this land for all."

"At the present time, yes," Thorne said, "but I was speaking with some travelers at Sylvester's last night, after you and the others had gone to bed. They tell me there's talk of the United States' government drawing up a treaty as early as this coming winter."

"What kind of treaty?"

"It's apparently going to demand that the Indians west of the Cascades give up their homes and leave. That includes the Nisqually, Puyallup and Steilacoom tribes from right around here. Even if the chiefs refuse to agree to the terms of the treaty, it's a bad sign of trouble to come."

"Isn't there something we can do?"

"Yes. We can get Naomi and Jacob delivered to the missionaries, as planned, and catch the first available ship bound for San Francisco."

With that, he dug in his heels and urged his mount down the trail toward the American settlement.

* * *

Following, yet keeping to the woods to avoid detection, Cyrus Satterfield reined in his horse, yawned and stretched.

The lone Indian who had remained with him snorted in disgust. "They get away. They go to fort. You see?"

"All I saw was that there were too many Nisquallies with them for us to chance another attempt. I'm not worried. I'll get them eventually."

"How you know which woman?"

"Simple. The one with the child has to be his mother. If I'm not sure when the time comes to take action, I'll kill them both and be done with it. Probably will, anyway."

"When? How? You go to fort?"

"I may, once I've scouted it out." He laughed at his companion's disconcerted expression. "I take it you're not coming with me that far?"

"No. Leschi go home, I go home."

"You never did tell me how you two are related."

"His mother Yakima. My father Yakima. Her brother."

"He knows you? Why didn't you *say* so? No wonder you didn't want to get close enough for him to see your face when we were chasing the woman and those fractious horses through the woods."

"Leschi a fool. He tillicum to King George men and Boston men. Make much peace. Patkanim say make war."

"And the rest of your tribe agrees, no doubt." He

patted the leather pouch containing the roots the Indian had found and pounded into a pulp for him. "All right. I have the arrow poison and I've paid you every bit you're going to get from me. I told you long ago I could handle this myself. Go on home. I don't need you."

"You see Leschi, you no tell him," the wiry Indian warned, "or poison arrow find your heart, too."

Cyrus was still chuckling derisively as he watched the other man wheel his horse and disappear into the dense forest.

In Charity's opinion, the mission complex looked more like a farm than it did a church. A surprised Mrs. White, who bore a striking, though graying, resemblance to Naomi, greeted her daughter with tears of joy. After brief introductions all around, she graciously ushered the entire party into her modest log home.

When Naomi didn't answer her mother's simple queries, Mrs. White turned her attention to Charity and the child. "I can't believe our Jacob has grown so big already. Naomi often wrote me about him."

"He is a big boy," Charity said. "Heavy, too." Reluctant to let him go, she nevertheless presented him to his grandmother. "This is your granny White, Jacob. Remember? I told you all about her."

The child hid his face next to Charity's neck and continued to cling to her.

His understanding grandmother backed off. "Give

him time. You've doubtless had a difficult trip." She nodded soberly toward her daughter. "What's wrong with my Naomi? Do you know?"

"I think so," Charity said, speaking quietly aside. "She was fine until her husband disappeared."

"Aaron? Where? When?"

While Charity remained in the parlor with Naomi and her mother to provide more details of their trials and tribulations, Thorne took Jacob outside into the yard.

"I want Mama," the boy whined.

"We'll go back in a few minutes. Aren't you anxious to meet your grandfather?"

"No."

Thorne huffed. "Well, nobody can accuse you of not being truthful, can they?" He saw a group of people hoeing in a nearby potato patch and ambled in that direction.

"Afternoon," the tallest man called. He removed his straw hat to mop his brow and Thorne could see that behind his thick, gray beard was the lighter but leathered skin of an aging settler.

"Hello. Mr. White?" Thorne asked.

"William White. That's me. What can I do for you?"

"I'd like you to meet your grandson," Thorne said with a grin. "This is Jacob Ashton."

"Well, well. God bless you for bringing him this far to see us." William offered his hand. "You must be Aaron."

"No. I'm his brother, Thorne. Half brother, to be

precise. I'm afraid Aaron has been missing since before we left San Francisco."

"Is our Naomi all right?" the older man immediately asked.

"She's here, too, if that's what you mean." Thorne was sizing up the other farm workers as he spoke. Most were Indian women but a few were older Nisqually men. None of them were looking at him with nearly as much friendliness as Leschi had demonstrated.

Thorne understood that Rev. White was understandably confused and concerned. "Naomi's in the house with your wife. I know you want to see her but can we go somewhere private to have a talk first?"

"Of course, but…"

"It will all make sense once I've told you the whole story. At least I hope it will," Thorne said. "We made it this far only by the grace of God."

The reverend nodded and began to smile as he led Thorne toward the rudimentary barn. "That's the only reason any of us are here, son. I'm glad to hear you giving proper credit to our Lord."

Thorne reentered the house accompanied by Naomi's father. Jacob ran straight to Charity and hopped up into her lap while Mrs. White, who insisted on being called by her given name of Nancy, made the rest of the introductions.

"Pleased to meet you, Rev. White," Charity said, smiling at him. "Nancy tells me you have a preaching planned for tomorrow. You must not postpone it on our account."

"Never have and never will," he replied. "It's not exactly our usual camp meeting, though. One of my flock is marrying a Nisqually woman over by Fort Steilacoom and I've been asked to conduct a brief Christian ceremony for them in addition to the one the Indians plan."

Charity was taken aback. "A wedding?"

"Yes. I've seen one other like it since we've been ministering here and it's truly fascinating. I know you'll enjoy seeing all the Indian folderol."

"Oh, we couldn't intrude," she said, hoping the excuse was enough to deter the preacher. The last wedding she had attended, with the exception of her sister's, was the sham of her own marriage. The notion of celebrating the nuptials of strangers did not sit well with her. It had been hard enough to muster the fortitude to attend Faith and Connell's ceremony back in California.

"Nonsense," the missionary said. "The more the merrier is the way these natives feel. I suspect they'll even invite some of the British from across the sound. I've been trying to encourage that whenever the occasion arose. We all need to learn to get along."

Charity sensed that Thorne was looking at her as if he were waiting for her to make the final decision. Oh, how she wished everyone would simply allow her to abstain from joining in any such festivities.

"We—we were going to leave very soon. Mr.

Blackwell has planned for it," she said, hedging as best she could. The silent plea she sent his way via her gaze was all she could politely accomplish. Unfortunately, Thorne did not seem to comprehend.

"There's no reason why we can't spare an extra day or two," he said. "Now that I see how much trouble Jacob is having settling in, I suspect it would be best to delay for a short while anyway." He smiled at the Whites. "And there may be questions you have that you've not thought to ask us yet. Miss Beal and I would be delighted to join you for the Indian wedding."

William White rubbed his hands together with delight. "Wonderful, wonderful. Folks will be coming from miles around. And afterward there will be a big, fancy meal. Nancy's been baking for days so she'll have something to offer the Nisquallies for their feast."

Sighing, Charity gave up searching for excuses. It was clear that they were all going to attend the wedding celebration whether she liked it or not. And she could understand why the Whites would want someone familiar to accompany Naomi and help them watch out for her, especially since she was going to be in a large crowd of strangers.

Plus, there was the problem of dear, bewildered little Jacob. Charity reiterated her vow to put his needs first. She would force herself to do whatever it took to help him adjust to becoming a permanent part of his grandparents' lives.

She blinked back unshed tears. Somehow, she

must help the child get over his undue attachment to her and Thorne, so he would be able to accept his new living arrangements happily.

The task sounded daunting but she knew she was up to anything. After all, she had been shot, withstood an Indian attack and lived through a fever that could easily have taken her life.

Given that, how hard could it be to spend a hour or two encouraging the child to be more friendly while they watched some nuptial festivities?

According to Rev. White, Fort Steilacoom had been founded on the site of a failed farm belonging to an English sheep rancher named Joseph Heath. William had explained that the fort's construction encompassed quite a few of Heath's original buildings, as well as added blockhouses for the protection of settlers. At strategic places along the solid perimeter fence there were also observation towers from which soldiers with rifles could easily defend their outpost if need be.

The Whites owned a spring wagon and several strong teams of workhorses which were much more like those Charity was used to seeing than the Indian ponies had been. She had assumed it would be more comfortable to ride to the fort in the wagon than on horseback until she'd been bounced over the rough, rutted road from Nisqually Flats for what had seemed like hours.

Poor Nancy had fretted about her cakes and pies

most of the way, worried they would be ruined by the buffeting. William had merely laughed and chided her for a lack of trust in the Lord.

When Nancy had snapped back, "It's not *God* I have a quarrel with. He's not driving this wagon through every pothole on the prairie," it had brought laughter all around and had further lightened Charity's anxiety. After all, she reasoned, she did believe in God. And she could see that she had been rescued by divine providence more than once, especially of late. Therefore, there was no reason why she should not be able to accept whatever Rev. White said or did during the ceremony.

I just hope and pray it doesn't make me remember my awful wedding too well, she added to herself. There were some people, some things, she might never be able to forgive or forget no matter how hard she tried. And, in the case of Ramsey Tucker, she had to admit she wasn't trying.

What she definitely did not want to hear was Bible teaching that might convince her that she was wrong to continue hating a man who was long dead. She wanted to loathe him. It was her right. He had abused her and she wasn't ever going to get over it.

Their arrival at Fort Steilacoom was heralded with such excitement Charity had little time to continue to brood. After she had helped Naomi and Jacob from the wagon, she put them both to work carrying Nancy's baked goods into one of the blockhouses that was being used to store the food the settlers were contributing for the coming feast. Tables inside were loaded with fish, clams, oysters and stews. Besides the usual side dishes of boiled potatoes, onions and bread, there were some strange-looking baked roots one of the soldiers had told her were camas, a wild staple food that the Indians loved.

It was hard for Charity to keep from staring at the other women who were present. Although they were dressed in calico instead of wearing triangular blankets over their shoulders and traditional bark skirts, their hair and skin were much darker than hers, leading her to conclude that these were the Indian wives of settlers and soldiers.

She didn't begrudge them their happiness, assuming they were content, she simply wondered how hard they had had to work to make the transition from their old way of life to this one. Such changes could not have been easy. In comparison, the challenges of her own life seemed almost simple.

Chatting with the women, Charity learned that some had undertaken more than a day's journey to get there. Others had rowed across the sound or had taken a steamship from as far away as Whidbey Island, to the north. Their fortitude was certainly commendable, as was their friendliness. When a few of them mentioned being born Nisqually, she was pleased to tell them she had met their chief.

"Leschi is very wise but not chief," a young woman explained. "His father, Sennatco, is one of our chiefs."

"Oh, I just assumed…"

The woman smiled. "I understand. Every man trust Leschi, even King George men and Bostons. He is friend to Dr. Tolmie, too."

"A medical doctor? Here?" Charity asked.

Some of the younger girls giggled. "Not here. At Hudson Bay Company. Dr. Tolmie runs it."

"Oh, I see. There's certainly a lot to learn. I'm sorry to say I won't be staying long enough to figure it all out. We're leaving very soon."

"You and husband?" She looked pointedly toward the place where Thorne was helping unhitch the horses.

Charity knew she was blushing because her cheeks felt as if they were aflame. "Mercy, no. We're not married."

"You go with him? Stay with him? Reverend White say that wrong. Should marry." She glanced around at the other Indian women in calico as they all nodded tacit agreement. "We no sin. We marry like Holy Bible teach."

"I'm not… Oh, never mind. You wouldn't understand," Charity said with a shake of her head.

"I will pray for you," the Indian said with a gentle smile. "You not sin. Yes?"

"Yes, I will not sin," Charity said, humoring her the way she would have a child.

Yet something in the woman's words, in her sincerity, kept nagging at the back of Charity's mind for the rest of the long afternoon and try as she might, she couldn't seem to shake the conviction.

Chapter Eighteen

Thorne took it upon himself to stick close and keep an eye on the women and Jacob while Rev. White made his way over to the temporary Indian encampment on the banks of the Nisqually River, a stone's throw from the fort.

The way Thorne understood it, Indian marriage was arranged by barter between the young woman's father and the intended groom. Acceptance of the proposal was partly dependent upon the offering of suitable, valuable gifts, such as horses and blankets.

Both factions had been dancing to Indian drums and singing, accompanied by a soldier's fiddle music, the previous night. Come morning, an official exchange of the last of the promised gifts was made between the groom's side and the bride's side before everyone gathered in parallel lines bordering an aisle of woven reed matting and awaited the appearance of the bride.

Thorne herded Charity and Jacob into place along the aisle while Nancy White looked after Naomi. Together, they stood quietly, respectfully, and listened to Rev. White speak an opening Christian prayer. Breathtaking, snowcapped peaks of the Cascades and a cloudless sky formed the perfect backdrop.

Thorne had noticed how quiet Charity had become of late and he was worried that she might be ailing again. When he had asked her, however, she had brushed off his concern as if she had never been racked by fever and delirium. Nevertheless, he held Jacob for her and stayed close enough to catch her if she swooned as a result of the hot sun or a return of her illness.

Charity pushed her bonnet off and let it hang at her back by its strings as an Indian maiden appeared and started to walk slowly, laboriously down the aisle. She was being escorted by several elderly Nisqually women. "Can that be the bride?" Charity asked aside.

"I assume so," Thorne bent closer to whisper.

"What has she got piled all over her?"

He stifled a chuckle before he answered, "Those blankets and shawls and all that finery are like her dowry. They'll take if off her and give it to the groom's people. Watch."

The Indians began to sing as other, younger women stripped away the layers of belongings to reveal a slim, lovely bride dressed in a tunic and leggings made of supple, white, fringed doeskin and trimmed with beads and tiny seashells. Instead of a veil, a closely woven hat of the same material as the mats sat atop her head. Her thick black braids hung below, entwined with thin strips of fur.

"Oh, my," Charity whispered. "She's beautiful."

"Aren't you glad you're here?"

"Yes. I must admit I am." Scowling, she glanced back at him a second time. "You knew I didn't want to come and you still refused to go along with my excuse. Why?"

"Because being here is the right thing to do."

He could tell she was less than pleased with his honest answer but he knew it was important that Charity be encouraged to share in the joy of matrimony, at least vicariously. It was no secret that her heart was badly scarred by her own marital mistake. He'd hoped that viewing the unusual ceremony would help her see that not all such unions were doomed to failure the way hers had been.

Charity sighed as she watched the elaborate ritual progress. Rev. White had completed his portion and had elicited the requisite "I dos." Then the Nisqually elders, all men, took turns speaking of the tribe's history and what they expected of the newly married couple.

The feast which followed featured the bride and groom eating from the same plate and sharing a drinking cup, which Nancy had explained was the Indian way of demonstrating that they were officially married. Besides the food the settlers had brought, there was fire-roasted salmon and trout, skewered bits of venison and elk and thick soups of clams and oysters.

Although Charity had not realized that personal trading among the women was also the custom, Nancy had provided extra ribbons and yard goods for her to offer the Nisquallies in exchange for shell jewelry and handwoven baskets.

By the end of the day Charity was the proud possessor of lovely trinkets and a small, finely woven basket in which to carry them. She showed her prizes to Nancy and saw the other woman's eyebrows arch.

"What's wrong?"

"Nothing," Nancy said, smiling. "I just think it's interesting, that's all. Where did you get the hat?"

Charity peered at her treasures. "Hat? What hat?"

Pointing, Nancy explained, "This isn't actually a basket. It's a married woman's brimless, reed hat like the one the bride had. Any woman who wears one is announcing to everyone that she's spoken for."

"Oh, dear." Charity blushed. "I know who gave it to me and now I know why. It seems that some of the Nisqually women think I'm rather scandalous for planning to travel back to San Francisco with Thorne. I assured them I was not going to sin but they are apparently convinced I'm a terrible person."

"You sacrificed to care for my daughter and grandson. I don't think you could do anything that would make me think less of you or of Mr. Blackwell. However, I have seen the way that poor man looks at you and I suspect your standoffishness is hurtful to him."

"Surely, you must be imagining things."

"May I speak freely, as a mother would?" Nancy asked, sobering and taking Charity's hand.

"Of course."

"My grandson loves you, as does his uncle, that much I know." She paused and cleared her throat, obviously struggling to continue. "I have seen a miniature of my daughter's husband. Aaron is fair, like Naomi, and it seems to me that Jacob…" Nancy's lower lip trembled.

Charity patted her hand to comfort her and waited for her to go on.

"My daughter is not the obedient child her father and I would have wished her to be," Nancy said. "She wrote to me shortly before she married Aaron Ashton and confessed a sin which I strongly suspect has haunted her ever since."

"I don't understand."

"Perhaps it would be better if you did not, but William and I have talked this over and have prayed about it. We have decided that I should tell you what I know and let you form your own conclusions. But before I explain, let me assure you that Naomi was once a very rebellious girl and was fully capable of seducing any man."

Charity stared, wondering, dreading, that Nancy might say what she, herself, had been thinking. More than once she had noticed the resemblance between

Jacob and Thorne, yet she had always set those suspicions aside, unwilling to entertain anything so shockingly unacceptable.

If she could have found her voice, she would have used it to silence the older woman. Unable to form coherent thoughts, let alone sentences, she merely gripped Nancy's hand more tightly and listened.

"Almost four years ago, when Naomi was engaged to Aaron Ashton, she—she consorted with another man."

"Thorne?" Charity's words were a hoarse whisper.

Clearly fighting tears, Nancy nodded. "Yes. And afterward, when she realized she was with child, she confessed it all to me in a letter. I don't think she ever told Aaron, let alone his brother, but now that I have seen the child, I have no doubts that Mr. Blackwell must be Jacob's father."

Thunderstruck, Charity just stood there, mute, and gazed at the distant, rugged mountains without seeing them. All the details, all the consternation, all the sibling rivalry and all of Naomi's guilty reactions suddenly made sense.

No wonder Thorne had seemed so overly concerned about Jacob's well-being. He wasn't his uncle, he was his father! Therefore, what about his feelings for Naomi? That was what hurt Charity the most. How could he have fooled her so completely? He'd seemed emotionally distant from Naomi and had pretended he was only looking after her because of a duty to his brother, while in reality he had fathered her only child.

Charity could not pretend she didn't care for one second longer. She'd been a fool. A stupid, gullible fool. How many times had she told herself it was insane to fall in love? Yet she had done it. That was the worst part of all this. She had fallen in love with a man who was unworthy of even the friendship and admiration she had bestowed. To *love* him, really love him, was an abomination.

Thrusting the basketry hat at Nancy, Charity broke away and ran, half-blinded by tears. She headed away from the encampment and toward the forest, the only place where she knew she'd find the privacy necessary to cry her heart out. She felt as if her best friend had abandoned her and that she had died as a result. Her hope *had.*

In a way, Thorne had died to her, too, she reasoned through her grief. He was a fraud. He had lied to her and led her on when all he'd really wanted was a nursemaid for his illegitimate son.

It didn't matter that Thorne had been planning to leave Naomi and Jacob behind in the territories and return to the sea. That made his perfidy even worse. Not only had he behaved in a beastly manner once, he was about to do it again by callously abandoning his child.

Cyrus Satterfield watched from the guard post inside the fort, smiled and blew smoke from his cigar. He'd wanted to draw at least one of the blond women away from her companions and it looked as if he was getting his wish, although he would have preferred that she'd taken the brat with her to save him the trouble of seeking it out later.

He sighted on the clump of cedars into which she had fled and lined it up with the Indian encampment so he could be certain of finding the right place once he had descended to ground level. She wouldn't get away from him this time. He not only had his rifle and pistol, he was also armed with the poison. It would be easy to steal an unattended arrow from one of the reveling Indians, poison its tip and use it to stab the woman to death. If he failed to get close enough for that, he'd simply shoot her, instead. The plan was foolproof.

And then he'd go back and take care of the other woman and the boy.

Thorne frowned as he scanned the assembled crowd. He was certain he'd seen Charity speaking with Nancy White a few minutes ago but at present he couldn't spot either of them.

Naomi had joined her father and seemed to be getting along all right, considering, so Thorne scooped up Jacob and headed their way.

William nodded and smiled a greeting. "Hello there. I wondered where everyone had gotten to."

"I was about to ask you the same thing," Thorne said. "I've lost track of Char…Miss Beal."

"Ah, I see." He patted the place next to him, opposite Naomi. "Why don't you two share our blanket and take a load off. I'm sure the women are fine."

"I don't know. It's not like Miss Beal to wander away alone." Thorne sat cross-legged on the blanket and held Jacob in his lap to keep him from running to join some older Indian boys who were chasing a playful, agile puppy through the milling throng of celebrants.

William nodded sagely. "I suspect Miss Beal wanted to do some serious thinking and praying."

"Why is that?" He didn't like the grave way the older man was looking at him. The perusal made him decidedly uncomfortable. When the reverend finally spoke, however, he understood the man's mood only too well.

"My dear wife has been telling your Charity a little about my daughter's past sins." Holding Naomi's hand in a show of support he pressed his lips together and nodded slowly, deliberately, as if he knew exactly what Thorne was thinking. "Our Naomi is many things but she has remained her mother's daughter. That's why she chose to bare her soul and ask our forgiveness before she went through with her marriage to your brother."

The older man directed a gentle, loving, knowing smile at Jacob. "We can see now that she was finally being totally truthful with us."

"I don't know what to say."

"You don't have to say a thing, son. 'All have sinned and come short of the glory of God.'"

Thorne hugged the child tighter. "I was not a Christian at the time. I don't know what I would have done if I had been."

"You are also a healthy young man. If my wife has the details right, you were not the instigator of the incident, nor were you unmoved by what you had done. She says you begged Naomi to marry you."

"Yes. I did," Thorne answered. He had been watching Naomi's blank expression and noted with relief that she seemed oblivious to what was being said. "My brother and I had a terrible quarrel when he saw her weeping afterward. As far as I know, she never admitted anything to him but Aaron must have known. How could he help but see the evidence in his son's face?"

"As have we all," White said. "Which brings me back to the matter of your Charity Beal."

"What about her?"

"Nancy has taken her aside and told her everything, discreetly I'm sure. If we are to carry out the plan we've been considering it was necessary that Charity be made aware of the entire story, first."

"No!" Thorne passed the child to William and leaped to his feet, scanning the crowd. "You don't know Charity the way I do. She won't be able to accept hearing something like that from anyone but me. I have to explain."

"Perhaps, if your intentions were as serious as I believe they are, you should have already done so."

"I was going to," Thorne said. "I was waiting for the right time."

"Then I suggest you find her. I'll watch the boy." He pointed. "Here comes Nancy. She should know where Charity has gone."

Thorne was beside himself. If Charity had been told all the sordid details of his past, she was probably never going to sit still long enough to listen to his pleas for forgiveness. He had no excuse for his behavior, nor had he ever had. It was just that he felt such news would have hurt less if it had come from him. Now that the damage was done, there was no telling how badly Charity had been hurt. Or what she might do or say as a result.

Running blindly, Charity tore through the mucky, grassy lowlands and straight into the forest. Her shoes were caked with mud, her skirt torn by brambles and her hands and face scratched, yet she pressed on.

The only pain she felt was in her heart and mind. "Oh, Thorne," she sobbed. "Why did you lie? Why didn't you tell me the truth?"

Because you would have hated me for it, came the unspoken answer.

Charity started to argue with herself, then realized that her conclusion was correct. She would have reacted in exactly the same way she was now, cut to the quick and blinded by tears.

Why weep for someone who was unworthy? Because, in her deepest heart and in spite of everything he may have done in the past, she was afraid she loved him still.

Gasping, she leaned against the trunk of a sturdy pine while trying to catch her breath. Why was she such a poor judge of men? She had idolized her father and he had abandoned her twice; once to go west in search of gold and again when he had as much as told her she wasn't important in his new life with Annabelle.

No thoughts of prior disappointments would be complete without considering Ramsey Tucker, too. He had taken advantage of her youth and inexperience to gain her trust and had abused her both physically and mentally while he was alive.

"But Thorne isn't like that," she argued, weeping and drawing in jerky breaths between sobs. "He isn't." He had always treated her kindly and fairly and with reserve, as a gentleman should. Even when she was half out of her mind with fever he had not done one thing that was out of line or could be construed as taking advantage of her.

If he's so perfect, why did he lie with Naomi? her broken heart asked. And why had he not made a clean break of his past?

That question brought her full circle to her original conclusion. When she barely knew him, such a confession would have kept her from agreeing to make the trip and care for the needy child. Later, when she had grown fond of Thorne, she would have been even less likely to accept his explanation no matter how fervently he had presented it.

Drawing another and another shuddering breath, Charity wiped her eyes on her sleeve and fought to calm herself. Other than a broken heart, a torn frock and a few scratches from her flight into the forest, she was physically unhurt. She would survive this trauma just as she had survived others. She would return to the Whites and act as if their news about Naomi and Thorne had not truly bothered her.

Will I be able to control my emotions when I look at him? she wondered. She doubted it but that did not negate her need to try to hold herself together, for her own sake as much as for that of Naomi's parents.

Oh, how she wished Nancy had not been so blunt. All the woman's words were awhirl in her mind, not making sense the way she wished they would. Nancy had said something about a plan and the necessity of revealing all, but for the life of her, Charity couldn't put those words into their original context.

Sniffling, she straightened, preparing to return to the wedding feast and face her disappointment. Turning in circles, she assessed the trees and blossoming blackberry thickets. It was impossible to tell which way she had come or even in which direction the fort lay.

Peering through the dense vegetation, she hoped to glimpse the snowcapped Cascade range and thereby get her bearings but the surrounding leaves and branches blotted out both the sun and the distant mountains. Worse, her headlong flight through the brush had not left enough damage to the vegetation to indicate her prior path.

Out of earthly options, she closed her eyes and laced her fingers together to pray for guidance. "Dear Heavenly Father, I've certainly gotten myself into a fine pickle, haven't I?" Her sigh punctuated the informal pleà. "Please? I know You must be tired of rescuing me but I really need some help? Which way should I go?"

When she opened her eyes and spotted a man coming toward her through the woods she was instantly relieved and deeply grateful.

"Thank you, God," she whispered, starting toward her rescuer with a wave of her arm.

In response, the man raised a rifle and pointed it directly at her.

She froze, incredulous. Surely he couldn't be planning to *shoot* her.

The click of the hammer being cocked echoed in the silence. He fitted the stock against his shoulder.

The muzzle flashed.

At that very instant, Charity ducked.

Chapter Nineteen

Thorne heard the resounding echo of the gunshot. He'd entered the forest where Nancy had told him to but had soon lost Charity's trail. He was a seaman, not a tracker, a lack of useful training which he now regretted.

He stiffened and waited for further sounds. None came to him. If the shooter was a local hunter, it seemed odd that he'd be out prowling the woods instead of attending the Nisqually celebration the way most folks were.

What if someone was after Charity, instead? What if they had shot her? Thorne's gut clenched and his head pounded. He had been praying for her safety and well-being ever since he had left the others and although he was as undeserving of grace as any man, he couldn't believe God would have ignored his plea on her behalf.

Pressing on toward the direction of the shot, he

prayed even more fervently. "Father, please help her. Keep her safe. Even if she never forgives me, please let me try to explain and tell her how much I love her. Please?"

Once again he paused and listened. Nothing. Disheartened, he lowered his gaze. There were no footprints visible on the dead leaves littering the ground but a spot of brightly colored cloth did catch his eye.

He waded amongst the thorny brambles until he was close enough to see that the torn scrap of fabric was of yellow calico and bore the same tiny, flowered pattern as Charity's skirt. Moreover, her discarded bonnet lay on the trail just beyond.

"That way." he said aloud. "She went that way. Thank the Lord."

Drawing a deep breath, Thorne shouted, "Charity," with all his might.

Instead of the reply he had expected, he heard her distant, panicky scream.

"Don't bother yelling," Cyrus said cynically. "It won't do you any good. It's just you and me. And pretty soon it will be just me."

"Did Louis Ashton send you?"

"What if he did?"

"I'm not the one you want. I'm not Mrs. Ashton," Charity insisted. "You must know that. Look at me. Don't you recognize me from San Francisco?"

"Maybe. Maybe not. I don't really care. I've been

watching you and that brat for hundreds of miles and if you're not his mama you sure act like you are. If I have my way, he'll be next."

"Jacob?" she gasped. "You wouldn't hurt an innocent child, would you?"

The assassin laughed. "I'd do in my own grandmother if it paid enough. Now, suppose you just hold still and let me get this over with."

The notion of standing there, as meek as a lamb, and letting him kill her was ridiculous. She didn't know what she was going to do or how she was going to escape but she did know she was not going to succumb without fighting back.

She cast around for a weapon. Anything would do. But other than a few fallen, rotten limbs there was nothing within reach that she could use for defense.

Trying to flee was also futile. Not only was she hampered by her voluminous skirts, she could already feel the creeping return of fatigue from the aftermath of her fever. She had spent—had wasted—what little strength she'd had in reserve and was now paying for her folly.

Backing away slowly, she decided to at least try to put a substantial tree or two between her and the evil man. That was when she noticed that he had propped his empty rifle against a rock instead of reloading it after he'd shot and missed. He was presently fiddling with an arrow though he had no bow that she could see. Surely, he didn't think he could seriously harm her if he couldn't fire that arrow.

Charity saw him open a pouch at his waist and stick the tip of the arrow into it with a stirring motion. Suddenly, she knew what he was planning. She'd heard tales of poisoned arrows from Leschi as they had traveled together and had felt sorry for the hapless game those arrows had brought down. Now, she feared she was about to find out exactly how the animals had felt as they had breathed their last.

No! her heart screamed. *I cannot die like this. Thorne will be devastated.*

The pure truth of that thought cleared her mind and forced her to see what her pride had made her keep denying. She *did* still love Thorne, deeply and irrevocably. In spite of his past, in spite of his deception, and in spite of, or perhaps because of, Jacob, she loved that stubborn, wonderful man with all her heart and soul and every ounce of her being.

"Get away from me. I told you, I'm not Naomi Ashton," she shouted at her attacker. "I'm Charity Beal. All I've been doing is helping take care of her and her little boy."

"That's really too bad. You see my problem, don't you? You know too much. I have no choice but to start with you and then go after the real Naomi, assuming you're not lying about who you are."

"I know who *you* are," Charity said, stalling for time. "You were a lodger at the Montgomery House hotel when the Ashtons were there."

"Now that you mention it, you do look a lot like that girl who worked at the hotel. She was paler and not nearly as able as you seem to be but I suppose it is possible."

"Of course it's possible, you dunderhead. I've been traveling with Naomi. We're both blond and blue-eyed and you've gotten us mixed up."

"Doesn't change anything," Cyrus drawled, displaying the arrow. "You hold still now and this will be over before you know it."

Charity fisted her hands of her hips. "I'll do nothing of the kind."

"Have it your way." With that he grasped the arrow as if it were a spear and started to close the short distance between them.

The gulp of air that filled her lungs was quickly expelled in a piercing shriek.

She turned at the same instant, hiked her skirts and ran for all she was worth.

Thorne heard Charity's scream. It made his hair stand on end. He braced, listened and heard more ruckus just ahead.

He shouted her name as he tore through the brush. If anything bad happened to her, he didn't know how he could go on, let alone find happiness again. She was everything to him. And she didn't even know it.

He broke through to a small clearing in time to see flashes of bright yellow moving in and out through the trees. *Thank God.* That was Charity's dress. He had almost overtaken her.

A man's coarse shout and muttered curses echoed

back to him and chilled his soul. As he had feared, Charity wasn't alone. Someone was pursuing her.

Thorne doubled his efforts, moving so swiftly he felt as if his boots barely touched the ground. He traveled on pure instinct, without thought, without plan, without the least concern for himself.

Low-hanging branches slapped and scraped his face. He felt nothing, cared about nothing except reaching the woman he loved.

He shouted, "Charity," at the top of his lungs.

On the returning breeze he heard the sweetest sound of all. She called back, "Thorne."

If his name had not been so heavily tinged with panic, he would have rejoiced.

Spent and gasping, Charity nevertheless managed to answer Thorne's summons. She knew then that if she did not yield to the painful stitch in her side, she would soon collapse into a helpless mound of vulnerability. She could not go on like this. She had to rest, if only for a moment. And now that she knew Thorne was close by, she took the chance that he'd arrive in time.

Whirling and holding up her hands to fend off her attacker, she hoped and prayed he wouldn't prick her skin with the poisoned point of the arrow.

Now that she'd looked back, however, she could tell that the heavyset man was as winded as she was. Maybe more so. His round face was ruddy and flushed and his breathing was ragged. Staggering, he halted, still brandishing the lethal arrow.

"It's not too late to walk away," Charity managed to say. Her sides were heaving as she bent forward at the waist. The taste of bile filled her throat and she feared she was about to lose all the food she had recently eaten.

"I'm not going nowhere, lady. I came all this way to do a job and I intend to finish it."

"How much did Louis Ashton pay you? We'll double it."

"We? We who? I don't see nobody else."

Charity glimpsed a flash of movement in the woods directly behind him and her heart leaped. She straightened and smiled as she said, "You will. Praise the Lord, you soon will."

Thorne hit the other man a solid body blow and knocked him facedown on the ground before he had a chance to turn around and fight back.

"Watch out for the arrow," Charity shouted. "It's poisoned."

Forewarned, Thorne grasped the feathered end and whipped the shaft from Satterfield's fist. The sharp blade passed across the assassin's palm, slicing into the meaty flesh.

With a yelp of pain and shock the man grabbed his wrist and rolled onto his back as Thorne jumped away. The portly man ended up lying against the gnarled roots of a tree where he began moaning and thrashing.

Thorne hesitated only a few seconds, waiting to be certain Cyrus wouldn't recover and renew his attack, then threw the arrow aside and went quickly to Charity.

Neither of them spoke. She stepped willingly into Thorne's strong embrace, slipped her arms around his waist and clung to him as if nothing on heaven or earth would ever separate them again.

He held her close, his cheek pressed against her silky hair, then guided her away from their now-helpless nemesis.

"Are you all right?" Thorne asked.

Charity nodded and looked up at him, unashamed of the fresh tears in her eyes. "I am now. That man said he wanted to kill me. And Jacob. All of us."

Tightening his hold on her, Thorne swallowed hard. "What did he have on that arrow?"

"Some kind of poison. I think he must have gotten it from the Indians."

"Dear God," Thorne said prayerfully. "That could be you lying back there."

"Or you. But it isn't." She was teetering between the shock of her narrow escape and the joy of being reunited with Thorne. Her knees were wobbly and her vision misty. "Once again, I have you to thank for coming to my rescue."

"No. We both have God to thank," he said, his voice choked with emotion. "I never stopped praying for you. All the time I was searching, I never stopped praying."

He placed one finger lightly beneath her chin and tilted her face up. "I know what Nancy told you. I was afraid I might never get the chance to say how sorry I was for keeping secrets when I should have spoken up."

"Is that all?" She was starting to smile.

"All? Isn't that enough?"

"No," she said tenderly as a solitary tear slid silently down her cheek. "You haven't told me you love me." Seeing his astonishment, she added, "I love *you*, you know."

"You do? Truly?"

"Truly. I didn't realize it until I'd nearly been sent to meet my Maker, but I finally figured it out. It doesn't matter to me what you did or didn't do in the past. If you've asked for the good Lord's forgiveness, that will be sufficient."

"I have. Many times over," Thorne said.

"Then I cannot deny you mine."

"Will you marry me?"

Charity was so overcome with happiness she was nearly unable to answer. The stricken look on Thorne's dear face as a result of her silence was what made her speak quickly and with assurance. "Yes. Oh, yes."

"When? Where?"

"Soon. Perhaps Rev. White will agree to perform the ceremony before we leave for California. I will be delighted to be able to inform my new Indian friends that I will not be tempted to sin."

She could tell by the strange way Thorne was looking at her that he was thoroughly confused.

Reaching up to pat his cheek, she grinned. "I have been instructed in the teachings of holy scripture by some caring Nisqually women. They also said they were praying for me because you and I were going to be traveling together and they were afraid I would be unable to resist your considerable charms."

To her delight, Thorne's face reddened and he began to give her his trademark, lopsided grin. "My charms?"

"Yes. In case you haven't noticed, I find you very appealing, Mr. Blackwell."

"Do you?" He arched an eyebrow. "In that case, perhaps we had best marry quickly, while you are still smitten."

"I suspect I will always be in love with you, sir."

Sobering, Thorne placed a tender kiss on her forehead before he said, "I know you were hurt before. I promise I will never harm you or frighten you. I would rather die than see you sad the way you used to be."

"It is a wonderment, but I don't fear you in the slightest," Charity said as she gazed into the depths of his dark eyes and saw all the love reflected there. "When we first met, I was not able to tolerate any man's touch without cringing, not even the innocent pat of my father's hand on mine."

Wrapping her arms around him once again and stepping into his embrace, she couldn't help smiling. "And now look at me."

"I am looking. And I think it would be best if we hurried back to the wedding feast," Thorne said, continuing to gaze at her with all the love he was feeling. "I made one big mistake in my life and I'm not about to make another."

"Did you love Naomi?" Charity felt his muscles tense beneath her touch.

"No. Never. I was acting the fool and I knew it, but I didn't have God's help resisting temptation the way you and I do now."

"I am resisting, truly I am. But it is not easy," she admitted with a blush. "If you will point me in the right direction, I will gladly rejoin the party. I can't wait to see the look on Nancy's and William's faces when we tell them we want to get married."

"Do you think they will be as surprised by it as you and I are?"

"I don't know about you," she said, taking his hand and letting him lead her away from the scene of mayhem. "But as Annabelle would say, I'm plum flabbergasted."

"Is that a good thing?"

Charity laughed again, positive she would never be happier no matter how long she lived. "It's a wonderment," she said. "A pure wonderment."

Their return to the wedding-feast grounds might have gone unnoticed if William had not insisted that some of the men from the fort form a search party. It was assembling and preparing to leave when Thorne and Charity stepped out of the woods together.

Thorne briefly explained what had occurred, then left Charity with the Whites and led a small group of soldiers back to take care of the body of Cyrus Satterfield.

The beaming smile Thorne saw on Charity's face when he returned made his heart lurch and his pulse

pound. Judging by the expressions of satisfaction
from the missionaries, they had been made aware of
Charity's and his decision to marry before they left
the territories.

William grabbed Thorne's hand before he could say
more than hello, and pumped it briskly. "Congratula-
tions, young man. Miss Beal told us everything."

"Will you perform the ceremony?"

"Of course. Would you like to make your nuptials
a part of this celebration?"

Thorne looked to Charity and saw her shake her
head. "I think it would be best if we did it back at
your place where there's less distraction, if you don't
mind," he said. "I want Charity to be comfortable."
He looked over at the child who had again insisted
that the future bride carry him. "And I want Jacob to
be a part of the wedding. I think we both do."

"Yes," she said.

As she tenderly kissed the child's cheek Thorne
could tell how badly she wished they didn't have to
part from him. That was the only sorrow in the fore-
seeable future. Someday, perhaps, they would have
a son of their own but that didn't mean it was going
to be easy to leave Jacob behind, even if it was for
his own good.

William cleared his throat and looked to his wife.
Nancy nodded assent to his unspoken question and
he began to speak.

"There is much unrest in these parts," White said.
"I know everything looks peaceful right now, while

everybody is celebrating, but there's an undercurrent of impending war with the Indians that can't be denied. Nancy and I will stay because it is our calling, and we will gladly assume the responsibility of our daughter's care, but we have decided that we cannot, in good conscience, let the child remain here with us. It's too dangerous. We are not able to guarantee his safety."

"What?" Frowning, Thorne stepped closer to Charity and put his arm around her shoulders to include both her and Jacob in a protective embrace.

"We know Jacob is dear to you both and since you are technically his father and Naomi is unable to even care for herself, let alone mind a lively little boy like him, we want you to take him. Make him your son, as he should be."

Charity was fighting tears. "But, he's not my son."

"He has already made the change, in his heart," Nancy said tenderly. "We've all seen it. He often calls you his mama, you know."

"Yes, but, he's just lonely and confused."

"And he needs a mother. He needs you. Of course, if you don't want him…"

"No! We do." She looked to Thorne. "Don't we?"

He could barely speak. "Yes. We do." More quietly he asked her, "Are you sure you don't mind?"

"I love him as my own. How could I mind? The only concern I have is what will happen to our plans if your brother returns and tries to reclaim him?"

"Don't worry. Before Aaron disappeared we had discussed the possibility of my taking custody of

Jacob if anything happened to him and Naomi. I'm sure, if we can prove to Louis that the child poses no threat of inheritance, he will gladly forget he was ever born."

"And will Aaron?"

Thorne nodded sadly. "Yes. If I have to confess the truth to him to finish this once and for all, then I will. I would rather have to live with my brother's lifelong hatred than jeopardize one hair on my son's head."

Looking down at Charity and the child in her arms, he knew he would gladly do whatever it took to guard and protect them for the rest of his life. And by the grace of God, he would succeed.

Epilogue

1858

Charity was glad Thorne had chosen to make San Francisco their permanent home, especially because doing so had brought her closer to her dear father and stepmother.

Though Thorne did occasionally sail on one of his vessels because he missed the sea, he had also built her a mansion overlooking the bay. When he was away she would often visit the "widow's walk" atop the roof and watch the harbor while she prayed for his safe return.

Jacob had matured to look even more like his father in the four years since they had unofficially adopted him. He was darkly handsome and every bit a Blackwell. So was his two-year-old baby sister, Mercy, who had been his shadow ever since she had first learned to toddle after him.

Charity sat knitting and smiled at her children as they played on the decorative Persian carpet at her feet. As usual, Jacob was acting the part of his sister's guardian, a role into which he had fallen as naturally as his father had when he had repeatedly saved Charity's life.

She was smiling and dreaming of Thorne when he appeared in the arched doorway of the parlor. Judging by the expression on his face he was privy to some news.

He waved a telegram and smiled. "Nancy White has accepted our invitation. She's coming to visit."

Charity laid aside her knitting and hurried across the room to see for herself. As she read the entire message she sighed. "That's wonderful. I was hoping she'd come. After all she's been through I'd wondered if she'd be up to it."

"I know. It had to be hard for her to give up her missionary work in the territories, but with William and Naomi both victims of the Puget Sound Indian war I can understand why she'd be ready for a change."

Charity slipped an arm around her husband's slim waist and stepped into the shelter of his embrace. "I was sad to read the news reports of Leschi's death, too. I had hoped his peacemaking would exempt him from the fighting."

"It should have," Thorne said soberly. "But in the end, I suppose he felt he had to side with his own people. I'm glad the hostilities are over. It's just too bad the war cost so many lives—on both sides."

His gaze went to his son. "Thank God, William was wise enough to send Jacob with us before the trouble started in earnest."

"I do thank God. Every day," Charity said. "And for you, too, husband. Do you think Nancy will agree to remain with us for a while? I'd love to have her here and I know she'll want to get to know her grandson better."

"We certainly have plenty of room," Thorne said.

"We do, don't we? And while we're on the subject, I think your mother might finally be ready to accept our invitation, too. You should ask her again."

Thorne hesitated, obviously mulling over the suggestion. "Really? After Louis died I thought she'd be eager to leave New York, but you know how she kept putting me off. What makes you believe she'd be willing to travel, now?"

"Because, as I told you when I received her last letter, I think she's finally accepted the fact she'll never see Aaron again. I know she was clinging to a faint hope he had somehow survived even though Louis was never able to locate any sign of him."

"And now she's let go? I hope you're right. I'll send her a telegram today. You're sure you don't mind having her and Nancy here at the same time?"

"Of course not. After all, they're both Jacob's grandmothers." She started to grin at him. "I am, however, beginning to feel as if I'm back in the hotel business."

Laughing, Thorne gave her a quick kiss before he said, "I promise you will not have to cook or make beds in this so-called hotel, my dear. We have servants for that, remember?"

"Yes, and you are spoiling me something awful," Charity replied. "I sometimes feel a bit useless. Since we're discussing changes, I suppose I should mention my plans to volunteer for several hours a week in the Orphan Asylum in the city." She watched his eyebrows arch in surprise but was pleased that he didn't argue.

"I worry about all those poor, lonely children," she went on as she gazed lovingly at her own. "There must be something I can do, besides donating money, to make their lives easier. I want to try."

Thorne pulled her closer and kissed her soundly before he said, "I would not expect anything less of you. And if you can manage to get Nancy White and my mother involved, too, I'm positive those motherless children will be blessed beyond imagination."

"What a wonderful idea! How did you get so smart?"

"The smartest thing I ever did was marry you," he said, smiling.

Charity returned his grin as she patted his cheek fondly and replied, "You have *never* been more right."

* * * * *

Dear Reader,

As I read pioneer accounts of the Indian uprising around Puget Sound in the mid-1850s I realized that, as usual, there was more than one side to the story. In the following details they all agree. The Medicine Creek Treaty, Dec. 1854, precipitated a war between the settlers and Indians. Leschi was a friendly, wise, Nisqually elder who tried to negotiate peace between the U.S. government and local tribes. He failed and was eventually tried twice for the same murder, which he denied committing. When he was finally convicted, the Army refused to execute him so he was hanged by civilian authorities in 1858.

Life does not always seem fair. Yet, as a Christian, I know that God is with me wherever I go or whatever I am called to do for His glory. I pray that you will seek and find the same sense of divine purpose that Charity discovers during her journey.

I love to hear from readers, by e-mail at VAL@ValerieHansen.com or at P.O. Box 13, Glencoe, AR, 72539. I'll do my best to answer as soon as I can and www.ValerieHansen.com will take you to my Internet site.

Blessings,

Valerie Hansen

QUESTIONS FOR DISCUSSION

1. Charity Beal has had a rough life before this story opens. Do you think her experiences have ruined her for good, as she first believes? Why or why not?

2. Charity makes up her mind that she will remain single for the rest of her life after her bad marriage. Is it sensible to make that final a decision at any age, let alone while still only sixteen years old?

3. Thorne was born and raised under trying circumstances. In spite of his efforts, he never felt accepted by his earthly father figure. Do you know anyone like that? Was it harder for them to accept their Heavenly Father's love?

4. Thorne has had an understandable falling-out with his half brother, Aaron. Is it reasonable for him to seek forgiveness? Will it be hard for Aaron to forgive him? What if Aaron is not a believer, too?

5. Naomi is reaping the results of her past sin. Is that fair? Even if she repents, shouldn't she be responsible for the consequences of what she's done?

6. Assuming Naomi has repented, why has her guilt overwhelmed her? Is it possible that although she

knows that God has forgiven her sin, she's unable to forgive herself? Isn't that pretty normal?

7. Some of the Indians are friendly to the settlers. Were they right to finally rebel when their way of life was in jeopardy? Wouldn't you feel the same way?

8. In retrospect, we see that the Nisqually and other tribes were doomed from the start. Was there anything the settlers could have done to help them more? Why was it seen as foolish to do so at that time in history?

9. Charity and Thorne take over as Jacob's parents in the end. Was that kind of unofficial adoption common in those days? (Yes!) Do you know if any of your ancestors were given homes in that way? My great-great-grandmother, Mina Alice Kelly was born a Ferguson and taken in by the Kelly family when her parents disappeared during the gold rush.

10. Charity mentions an "Orphan Asylum" which actually existed in old San Francisco. What do we do these days? In spite of a few stories of problems within the system, isn't foster care a better option for children without parents than being institutionalized? How many other children do you think a loving person like Charity might decide to adopt?